Praise for

Vulnerable

Here's what some readers have to say about the first book in the
McIntyre Security Bodyguard Series...

"I can't even begin to explain how much I loved this book! The
plot, your writing style, the dialogue and OMG those vivid
descriptions of the characters and the setting were so AMAZING!"
– Dominique

"I just couldn't put it down. The first few pages took my breath
away. I realized I had stumbled upon someone truly gifted at
writing. " – Amanda

"*Vulnerable* is an entertaining, readable erotic romance with a
touch of thriller adding to the tension. Fans of the *Fifty Shades*
series will enjoy the story of wildly rich and amazingly sexy Shane
and his newfound love, the young, innocent Beth, who needs his
protection." – Sheila

"I freaking love it! I NEED book 2 now!!!" – Laura

"Shane is my kind of hero. I loved this book. I am anxiously
waiting for the next books in this series." – Tracy

Praise for
Fearless

Here's what some readers have to say about the
second book in the McIntyre Security Bodyguard Series...

"Fearless is officially my favourite book of the year. I adore April
Wilson's writing and this book is the perfect continuation to the
McIntyre Security Bodyguard Series."
– Alice Laybourne, Lunalandbooks

"I highly recommend for a read that will provide nail biting
suspense along with window fogging steam and
sigh worthy romance."
– Catherine Bibby of Rochelle's Reviews

Books by April Wilson

McIntyre Security Bodyguard Series:

Vulnerable

Fearless

Shane — a novella

Broken

Shattered

Imperfect

Ruined

Hostage

Redeemed

Marry Me — a novella

Snowbound — a novella

Regret

With This Ring — a novella

plus lots more coming...

With This Ring

McIntyre Security Inc.
Bodyguard Series
Book 12

BY

APRIL WILSON

This novel is a work of fiction. All places and locations mentioned in it are used fictitiously. The names of characters and places are figments of the author's imagination. Any resemblance to real people or real places is purely a coincidence.

Wilson Publishing
P.O. Box 292913
Dayton, OH 45429
www.aprilwilsonauthor.com

Visit www.aprilwilsonauthor.com to sign up for the author's e-mail newsletter to be notified about upcoming releases.

ISBN: 9781688119734

Published in the United States of America
First Printing August 2019

Dedication

For Lori, my sister and best friend

1

Annie Elliot
(soon to be Annie McIntyre)

I'm getting married today to the love of my life. To the boy I fell in love with years ago, back in high school. To the boy I lost. By a twist of fate, we found each other again nine months ago, and we've been given a second chance.

Of course he's no longer a boy. He's a grown man... and what a fine man he turned out to be.

I'm not surprised.

He's a *McIntyre*.

Jake's arm snakes around my waist and his hand settles possessively on my burgeoning belly, which is home to our twin baby girls who are due to arrive any day now. Maybe any *hour*. I just hope they wait until after the wedding ceremony to make their appearance. I waited over a decade to make this man mine, so there's no way I'm going to miss my own wedding.

Today is *our* day. It's March 5, the day we should have gotten married over a decade ago. We never got to have our wedding, as our lives took very different turns. But now we have another chance, and I'm determined to say 'I do' on March 5, just like we'd planned. As they say, better late than never.

"Jake? Are you awake?"

He presses his face into my hair and whispers back with a hint of protest. "No."

We spent the night at Jake's brother's estate in Kenilworth, just north of Chicago. This is where the wedding will take place this afternoon. This home holds a special place in our hearts—it's here that Jake and I reconnected after years of separation. It's where we found each other again. It's where our bodies and minds and hearts began the process of healing.

This is the very same bed where our twin baby girls were conceived, quite by accident, I might add. We let the excitement of the moment go to our heads and forgot to use protection. All it took was once, and... oops.

But neither of us really minded. Jake comes from a family of seven kids, and I'm an only child. We both want a large family.

We drove up from our new home in Lincoln Park the evening before, along with my five-year-old son, Aiden, and Jake's entire family, to spend the evening together in a pre-celebration of our nuptials.

Wide awake, I glance at the digital clock beside the bed. "It's six-thirty."

"Too early," he grumbles, tightening his hold on me. "Go back to sleep."

I chuckle. Sometimes, like now, this former heavyweight boxer is just a big baby. "I can't. I have to pee."

With a groan, he presses a kiss to the back of my head and releases me so I can haul my awkwardly cumbersome and naked body out of bed and waddle into our private bathroom.

After relieving my bladder, I stand at the sink to wash my hands and brush my teeth. I stare in amazement at my distended belly, heavy with child—children, rather. Faint, silvery stretchmarks are a testament to how my body has changed to accommodate my pregnancy. In the beginning, I was self-conscious about the marks, but not now. Jake has gone out of his way to praise my body for its miraculous ability to make babies.

I stretch my aching body, grimacing at the discomfort radiating from the base of my spine. Carrying twins has certainly put a lot of pressure on my back. I wasn't nearly this big when I was pregnant with Aiden.

I squint at my reflection in the mirror, frowning when I see what a tangled mess my hair is. No amount of finger-combing is going to help this. But I'm not worried. Jake's eldest sister, Sophie, has offered to do my hair and make-up today. A highly sought-after interior designer, Sophie is a genius when it comes to all things girly and glamorous.

I realize Jake's whispering from the bedroom.

"Elliot, come back to bed!"

Chilled, I return to bed, sliding beneath the covers to snuggle up to his warm body. He naturally runs hot, and I love it because I'm always cold.

When I slip my arms around his waist, he shudders. "Jesus, woman, you're freezing!"

Smiling, I burrow closer, my nose pressed against his broad chest, and let his warmth seep into me. "Mmm. Not anymore."

His masculine scent fills my senses, teasing me as it makes my nerve endings come alive. Pregnancy has done wonderful things for my sex drive. Sometimes I just can't get enough of him. And he hasn't complained once.

When I press my lips to the center of his chest, he groans softly and pulls me closer... at least as close as my rounded abdomen will allow. It's hard to cuddle when there's a beach ball between you.

Pregnancy has made sex a bit of a logistical challenge, but Jake is nothing if not resourceful. He rolls me to my other side, so that I'm facing away from him. "We don't have much time," he says, his voice heavy with sleep. "Once everyone's up, I won't get another moment alone with you all day."

His hand skims down my back, over my bare butt cheek, and he slides his fingers between my legs from behind, gently exploring. He groans. "You're so wet."

His touch makes me shiver. "Jake."

He lifts my leg and slides his thigh between mine, and soon I feel the firm pressure of his erection nudging my opening. As he presses into me, so slowly, so exquisitely, he trails soft kisses along my sensitive bare shoulder.

Now it's my turn to groan as I push back against him, deepening the penetration.

He presses his face into the crook of my neck and shoulder. "Oh, God."

His rough voice sinks into me, deep and resonant, and I feel my body soften for him, stretching to accommodate his impressive size.

He sinks a little deeper. "I'm marrying you today," he whispers against my throat.

His fingers slide around in front of me, and he teases my clitoris. "We'll be joined together..." His erection sinks deeper into me. "...as man and wife..." And deeper still, one inch at a time. "...'til death do us part."

When he's fully seated, his loins nestled against my bottom, I gasp, completely overwhelmed by the delicious sense of fullness. When he's inside me like this, he takes me over, not just literally, but figuratively as well. My mind goes blank, and all that registers is how perfectly he feels inside me.

As he starts to move, my body flushes with heat and my pulse flutters. I clamp down on his erection, loving the feel of him inside me.

He groans. "Jesus, Elliot, you're killing me."

The sheer satisfaction in his voice brings a knot to my throat and tears to my eyes. After having suffered through a miserable, abusive first marriage—I never knew when Ted was going to get angry and fly off the handle—I find the prospect of soon being married to *this* man, this gentle giant, too good to be true.

Jake pulls out and sinks back in, starting up a slow, tantalizing rhythm that teases my nerve endings and sends my pulse racing. As he thrusts, his warm hand cups my belly, his long fingers splayed wide. I may be as big as a house right now, but he makes me feel beautiful. His possessiveness gives me confidence, and his gentle thoughtfulness makes me want to cry.

As he thrusts slowly in and out, his finger is relentless as it teases my clitoris, rubbing faster and faster and driving my pleasure higher. I'm drenched with arousal, and his finger slides easily over the tiny little bundle of nerves.

My breath shallows. "Jake!"

He presses his mouth against my shoulder and gently sucks.

"Don't give me a hickey there!" I warn in a breathless pant. "It'll show."

"I'm okay with that. I want everyone to know you're mine."

I reach back to swat his muscular butt. "Everyone will see it! Your parents will see it!"

He chuckles as he kisses his way to the back of my neck. "Fine. I'll put it where it doesn't show."

He continues thrusting, his rhythm slow and steady, which he knows drives me wild. I reach back and grip his thigh, digging my nails gently into his thick muscles. Between his thrusts and his fingers on my clitoris, it doesn't take me long to implode. As my orgasm hits hard, I press my face into a pillow to muffle my cries.

He follows almost immediately after me, thrusting deeply and holding himself still as he erupts inside me. "God!" he growls, pressing his hot face into the crook of my neck. His entire body is wracked with violent shudders as he comes, his breath hot and heavy on my damp skin. "Elliot!"

I reach back and hold him to me as his orgasm wanes. He wraps his arms around me, clutching me to him. Since we found our way back to each other, we've been inseparable and insatiable. I think we're both a little bit afraid that if we blink, it'll all go away, as if it's all been just a dream.

We're both breathing heavily as we lie here together, our bodies still joined. As his penis softens, he slips out. I can feel the warm trickle of his come on my thighs.

He turns me to face him and cups my chin. "I love you, Annie." He looks me directly in the eye as he says that, and it's not just a simple declaration of love. It's a promise. A vow.

My throat tightens. "I love you, too."

We lost so many years, and we've both shed so many tears. I still don't fully understand what happened back then. I know my parents interfered in our relationship. They led me to believe that Jake had started seeing other girls while I was away at Harvard. And they led him to believe that I'd moved on, that I was dating other guys at the university. But still, *we* let this happen to us.

We were naive and easily swayed, as young people often are, but that's no excuse. We suffered so much, and we'll always regret that we let this happen to us.

"Hey, no tears," he says as he kisses the tip of my nose. "Today's a happy day."

It's the day we join hands to declare ourselves husband and wife to all the world. Today, Aiden gains a stepfather who has done far more for him in a matter of *months* than his own abusive one ever did.

Jake nuzzles the crook of my neck. "I, Jacob Andrew McIntyre, take thee, Anne Margaret Elliot, to be my lawfully bedded wife—"

Laughing, I reach back and swat his butt cheek. "Don't you dare—"

My retort is interrupted by a quiet knock on our door, followed by a very loud whisper.

"Mommy! Are you awake?"

Jake rolls to his back with a groan. "And... now grown-up time is over."

"Shh!" I whisper, laughing. Then, louder, I say, "Come on in, sweetie."

The door opens tentatively, and Aiden slips inside, closing it behind him. He races for the bed and climbs on top of the covers, settling between us. He sighs dramatically. "I can't sleep."

"Why is that?" I ask him.

"I'm too excited! We're getting married today."

"Yes, we are," Jake says, hauling both me and Aiden into his arms. "The three of us officially, legally, become a family today."

Aiden looks at Jake. "You'll be my dad for real then?"

"You bet." Jake ruffles Aiden's short, spiky brown hair. "After today, I can officially adopt you."

"Then I'll be Aiden McIntyre, instead of Aiden Patterson?"

"That's right."

"And you'll be my baby sisters' dad, too?"

Jake mock-growls as he tickles Aiden. "Yes, I'll be their dad too. Hey, it's awfully early for you to be full of so many questions. Are you sure you don't want to go back to bed and get some more shut-eye?"

Aiden sits up. "I'm not sleepy. I'm hungry."

It looks like snuggle time is definitely over. "Are my two favorite guys ready to go downstairs for breakfast?"

Aiden surges to his feet and jumps on the bed. "Yay! Pancakes! Elly said she's making pancakes for breakfast."

Grumbling good-naturedly, Jake slips out of bed and strolls naked to the bathroom.

Aiden drops to his knees on the bed and howls with laughter.

"What's so funny?" I ask him.

He points at Jake's bare backside as he disappears into the bathroom. "Daddy's naked!"

* * *

After taking a quick shower, Jake returns to the bedroom and pulls on a pair of black boxer-briefs, jeans, and a T-shirt. He ruffles Aiden's hair as he meets my gaze. "I'll get this guy dressed while you shower."

Aiden jumps to his feet and raises his arms eagerly. "Can I have a piggy-back ride? Please?"

Jake turns his back to Aiden, who climbs on like a little monkey, and the two of them gallop out of the room.

Once they're gone, I heave myself out of bed once more and head to the bathroom for a shower. The spray of hot water feels wonderful on my aching back, and for a moment I stand there and let the water work its magic. Then I quickly wash and shampoo my hair. I even shave again so my legs will be silky soft tonight on my honeymoon.

It's not until I'm standing at the sink drying my hair that the first contraction hits me.

Oh, no! No, no, no!

Doubling over, I grab hold of the bathroom counter and pant through the contraction, just like I learned in birthing class. When it passes a moment later, I straighten hesitantly and stare at my pale face in the mirror.

I'm in labor.

I'm going to give birth to two baby girls.

But not until after we're married, damn it!

"Ready, honey?" Jake calls from the bedroom.

"Just a sec!" I slip on my maternity robe before leaving the bathroom and hastening through the bedroom to our walk-in closet.

Aiden is seated beside Jake on the bed, too engrossed in his favorite toy—Stevie the Stegosaurus—to pay me much attention. "I'll be ready in a minute."

Once safely inside the closet, I lean against the door and will my heart rate to calm down. *I can do this.* It's only a few hours until the ceremony starts.

After I pull on a clean pair of panties, a maternity sundress, and sandals, I paste a smile on my face in an effort to hide the massive lump of anxiety that has taken up residence in my chest.

Jake can't know!

If he realizes I'm in labor, he'll whisk me off to the hospital, and I am *not* going to miss my own wedding. I've waited my whole life for this day—March 5th—and I'm not going to miss it. Today is *our* day. I'm not going to let this chance slip away from me.

* * *

It's seven-thirty when the three of us head downstairs to the dining room. Shane's housekeeper, Elly, already has a fantastic breakfast laid out on the buffet.

"Hi, Elly!" Aiden calls out as he bounds into the room. "I'm starving to death!"

Elly laughs as she pats his head. "Then you've come to the right place. Have a seat, honey, and I'll make up a plate for you." She gives me a smile. "You look radiant this morning, Annie."

Jake pulls out a chair for me, and after I'm seated, he kisses the top of my head. "She *is* radiant."

Jake brings me a plate, and I force myself to eat. It's difficult, though, as I'm a nervous wreck. Maybe what I felt earlier was just a Braxton-Hicks contraction. Maybe I'm worrying about nothing. But I am at thirty-eight weeks now, and I'm carrying twins, which is a huge risk factor for preterm labor. It's entirely possible. Maybe Jake's sister-in-law, Beth, might know. Or Jake's mom, Bridget.

Aiden's busy chatting with Elly about the horses. It was dark when we arrived last night, too late for Jake to take Aiden out to see them.

By the time Jake is seated with his own breakfast, Aiden has nearly polished off a stack of pancakes. "Daddy, can we go see the horses?"

"Sure, pal. After we eat, I'll take you out to the barn. Unless

Mommy needs me for something?" He looks to me for confirmation.

"That sounds like a great idea," I say. Keeping Jake distracted before the ceremony is a good thing.

Suddenly, my abdomen draws tight, my muscles contracting. I try not to react, but my heart is hammering in my chest. It feels like there's a band tightening around my belly, so tight it's hard to breathe. I blow out a slow breath as I count the seconds.

Jake watches me intently. "Is everything okay?"

I force a smile. "Yes, fine."

He looks pensive as he lays his hand on the back of my neck and gently massages my muscles. "You'd tell me if you weren't feeling well, right?"

My heart skips a beat, and I wonder if I've already given myself away. I lay my hand on his rock-hard thigh. "I'm fine, sweetie."

To distract him, I snag his hand and bring it to my lips to kiss, hoping he didn't notice that I never answered his question. I would never lie to Jake, but maybe this once it's okay if I omit a tiny bit of information.

$\backsim$ 2

Annie

After we finish eating, Jake gets Aiden ready to go outside to look at the horses. As they put on their coats and gloves, Jake watches me closely. The man's professional expertise is surveillance, and he has a highly developed sense of intuition when it comes to reading body language. The less he sees of me right now, the better, at least until I figure out whether I'm truly in labor or not.

When Elly disappears through the door to the adjoining kitchen, I collect our dirty dishes from the table and carry them to her.

"You don't have to do that, honey." She rushes to take the plates from me. "This is your special day. You shouldn't be doing housework."

I smile gratefully. "You take such good care of us. The least I can do is help out."

I head back into the dining room just as Jake's parents, Bridget and Calum, breeze in looking more than a bit flushed. Bridget's fair, freckled complexion is rosy from exertion, her strawberry-blonde hair pulled up in a wind-blown ponytail. Calum takes Bridget's coat and hangs it on the back of an empty chair.

As she sits, Bridget spots me and smiles. "Hello, darling. It's beautiful outside. We just walked down to the lake. Have you eaten yet?"

"I ate a few minutes ago with Jake and Aiden."

"We saw them just now," she says. "They were on their way out to the barn."

Calum pours a cup of coffee. "That boy is growing like a weed."

I'm grateful to Bridget and Calum for the way they've welcomed me and my son into their tight-knit family. They shower him with attention and treat him just as if he was their own grandson.

Calum hands the coffee to Bridget and kisses the top of her head. "If you ladies don't mind, I think I'll join Jake and Aiden outside."

"Go right ahead, honey," Bridget says, shooing her husband out the door.

Of all the women here today, Bridget has the most experience with pregnancy—after all, she's the mother of seven. I take a seat next to her. "Can I speak to you? In private?"

She looks surprised. "Of course. What is it, honey?"

At that moment, one of the babies kicks, and my hand goes automatically to my rounded belly. I don't know which little girl it was who just made her presence known. All I know is that I'm anxious for them to be born, so I can hold them in my arms. Just not today, I hope. I want to marry their father first.

Meeting Bridget's curious gaze, I get right to the point. "I've had two contractions this morning."

Her blue eyes widen. "I see."

"They weren't painful, but they were definitely contractions."

"How long did they last?"

"Around twenty or thirty seconds each. How do I know if I'm in labor, or if they're Braxton-Hicks contractions?"

"Well, you have to time them. If they're regular and start coming sooner, lasting longer, they're probably real contractions. If you've only had two, I think it's too soon to tell. Have you told Jake?"

I shake my head. "No! If he thought I was in labor, he'd take me straight to the hospital, and I want to get married first. It's only a few hours until the ceremony. Surely I can hold out that long before sounding an alarm."

Bridget lays her hand on my back. "How about if we just keep a close eye on things and see how the day goes?"

I'm so relieved I could cry. "Thank you."

Our attention is suddenly diverted by the sound of voices in the foyer. We check to see who has arrived. It's my parents.

I'm happy to see my father. He's apologized to both me and Jake for his role in breaking us up after high school, but my mother... she's not been so repentant. She still holds a terrible grudge against Jake, and I have no idea why.

Jake saved my father's life and mine—quite literally—when Ted attacked us in the hospital after my father's heart attack. And still my mother treats him like he's the enemy. Frankly, I'm surprised she even came today. I wasn't sure if she would.

"Shall we go say hello?" Bridget says, linking her elbow with mine.

Reluctantly, I nod. I just hope my mother is on her best behavior and is courteous to Jake's family.

My parents are standing just inside the door, looking a bit out of place and unsure.

"You're here!" I say. "I'm glad you made it." It's strange that meeting my own parents has become awkward.

"Hello, honey," my dad says, holding out his arms to me. He's recovered well from his heart attack. I know he's been eating better and exercising, and he's even lost a few pounds. His complexion appears much healthier.

We hug, and he laughs when my belly gets in the way. "I can't believe I'm about to become a grandfather again."

When he releases me, I turn to my mother. "Hi, Mom."

"Hello, Annie," she says, sounding sullen.

I'm guessing my dad pressured her into coming today.

She glances around the foyer, and I wonder who she's looking for. Her grandson, perhaps?

"Aiden's outside," I say. "Jake took him to see the horses."

She meets my gaze. "Please tell me there's fresh coffee."

"Yes, Roberta," Bridget says, pointing to the dining room. "Right in there."

My heart sinks as my mother disappears into the dining room without another word. I don't know what I was expecting, but it wasn't this. I was hoping she'd at least try to be cordial.

My dad pats my back. "I think I'll walk out to the barn and say hello to Jake and Aiden."

I give my dad a parting smile, grateful that he's making a concerted effort to be sociable. My mother—not so much. Compared to the McIntyres, my family is so dysfunctional. It always has been. And I'm not even sure why. I just know that it revolves around my mother and her blatant bitterness.

"Come upstairs, darling," Bridget says, as she links her arm with mine. "Let's go check on your dress."

My dress, which had to be altered to accommodate my pregnancy, is pressed and ready, hanging in a garment bag in our closet. It's not a typical wedding gown, but when I saw it on the rack at the shop, I knew it was what I wanted. The short-sleeved bodice is a shimmering champagne silk, and the full skirt is a lovely pale shade of peach. Peach is my favorite color. My wedding bouquet is a mix of peach roses and cream-colored peonies.

As we head up the staircase, Beth and Shane and Luke are just coming down.

"Good morning," Beth says. "Where are you two going?"

"We're going upstairs to check on my dress," I say. "Why don't you join us?"

Bridget nods eagerly. "Great idea! Come upstairs with us." She gives me a conspiratorial wink, and I have to bite my lip to keep from laughing.

"I'd love to." Beth hands Luke to Shane. "Can you give him his breakfast?"

As the three of us enter my suite, Bridget closes the door.

Beth props her hands on her hips. "All right, what's really going on?"

I blurt out the truth. "I might be in labor."

Beth's blue-green eyes widen. "Are you serious?"

"Yes," Bridget says. "And since you're the one with the most recent childbirth experience, we thought you might know. How do you tell the difference between Braxton-Hicks contractions and real ones?"

"I'm not entirely sure." Beth pulls her phone out of her pocket. "I'll look it up." While she's scanning the information on her screen, she says, "Does Jake know?"

"No," I say. "And he can't know until *after* the wedding ceremony. Please don't say anything."

There's a knock at the door, and we all freeze.

I open the door to find Molly standing there, Jamie's girlfriend. "Hi, guys," she says, peering into the room. "Shane said you were all up here. Mind if I join you?"

I stand aside to let her enter. "Please, come in and join the party."

Molly scans the room, studying our apprehensive expressions. "Is everything okay?"

Right at that moment, another contraction begins, starting with a mild wave of pressure that radiates outward from my abdomen. "Oof," I gasp, pressing my hands to my belly. I walk backward until I reach the bed and sit.

"When was the last one?" Beth says, reading from her phone. "It says here that real contractions follow a pattern. The Braxton-Hicks contractions occur more randomly. We need to time them."

I think back. "The last one was during breakfast. That was about thirty minutes ago."

"And the one before that?" Bridget says.

"Here in my room. About an hour ago."

Beth frowns. "That doesn't sound good. It definitely sounds like there's a pattern. I think they might be the real thing."

Molly pales as she asks me, "Are you in labor?"

I nod. "I might be."

"Does Jake know?" she says.

"No!" Bridget, Beth, and I say simultaneously.

"He can't know," I explain. "If he did, he'd make me go straight to the hospital."

"She doesn't want to miss her wedding," Bridget says to Molly.

I let out a long breath as the wave passes. "The ceremony is in three hours. I just have to make it until then. I was in labor with Aiden for *eighteen* hours. Surely I can last a little while longer before I have to go to the hospital."

"At least Jason Miller's coming today," Beth says.

Bridget looks confused. "Who?"

"Jason," Molly says. "He works for Shane—he's the one who delivered Luke. He's a former paramedic."

"Oh, good lord." Bridget presses her hand to her chest. "It had better not come to that."

We all jump when there's yet another knock.

Molly opens the door this time and steps back to admit Jake's eldest sister, Sophie.

"Hi, everyone," Sophie says, scanning the room. Her eyes light on me. "I thought you might want to get started on hair and make-up." A hint of a frown mars her lovely face as she studies me. "Is everything okay?"

Sophie is tall for a woman, nearly six feet tall, and statuesque. She has a killer hour-glass full figure and the confidence to go with it. With her hair the color of fine dark chocolate and dark eyes, she's gorgeous and sophisticated and worldly... everything I'm not.

Letting out a heavy sigh, I confess. "I think I'm in labor."

Sophie's expressive eyes reflect much of what we're all feeling. "Oh, my. Does Jake know?"

"No!" we all exclaim in unison.

3

Jake

Dad and I stand leaning against a stall door as we watch Aiden climbing stacks of straw bales. After paying a visit to the horses, we opted to come inside the barn to get out of the cold. Aiden loves playing in the barn, and I can't say I blame him. It's a kid's wonderland.

"Be careful!" I holler at him as he scampers up the ladder to the hay loft.

"I'm proud of you, son," Dad says, standing at my side, shoulder to shoulder. "I remember the day you told me you were going to marry Annie Elliot, back when you were still in high school. It may have taken longer than you'd planned, but you made it happen."

I smile, remembering the first time I kissed Annie here in this barn. "It's not every day a man gets a second chance with his first love."

"Jake, look at me!" Aiden calls down from the loft. He waves at us from his perch on a stack of three hay bales.

I wave back. "That's high enough, pal." I head for the ladder, intending to join him up there, when the door opens and in walks Frank Elliot.

"Hello, Jake," he says, closing the door behind him to keep out the blustery March wind. He stomps his snowy boots and rubs his hands together to generate some warmth.

I nod to him in greeting. "Hi, Frank." Ever since the hospital incident, Frank's been more than decent with me. I wish I could say the same for Annie's dragon of a mother.

Frank offers a hand to my dad. "Calum."

Dad shakes his hand. "Glad you could make it today, Frank."

"I wouldn't miss it for the world," Frank says. "Annie's happiness is all that matters to me."

I nod. "Too bad your wife doesn't feel the same way."

Frank scowls. "I'm sorry about that, son. I really am."

I've been trying not to hold a grudge against Annie's parents for what they did to us so long ago. They're her parents, after all. We need to make peace with them. They're Aiden's grandparents, and they'll be the grandparents of our baby girls. It hasn't been easy. Of course we have to bear some of the blame. We allowed them to manipulate us.

Annie ended up married to a narcissistic asshole who abused her emotionally and physically. When he started in on their toddler son, Aiden, that was the final straw for Annie. She left Ted Patterson. But the threats didn't stop, and that's how I came back into the picture.

Frank hired McIntyre Security—my brother Shane's firm—to protect Annie from her ex-husband, restraining order notwithstanding, and Shane assigned me to the case. It wasn't until after Ted tried to kill Annie that Frank confessed that he'd hoped all along that putting me and Annie in the same room together would fix all the old wrongs.

He was right, of course. The moment I laid eyes on Annie, all the years we spent apart simply melted away, and those old feelings came rushing back. It wasn't long before she was back in my arms where she belonged.

"Hi, Grandpa Frank!" Aiden yells down from the loft. "Come up here and see how high it is!"

I spot Frank as he climbs the narrow wooden ladder up to the loft. It wouldn't do for me to let Annie's father fall and break his neck on our wedding day. I follow him up, and we join Aiden on the hay bales.

"Look!" Aiden says, pointing at a window. "We can see the horses from here!"

Out in the pasture is Elly's little herd... five in all, including a one-year-old colt.

"When I'm big, I'm going to learn how to ride a horse. Elly said she'd teach me."

While Aiden and Frank admire the horses and the view from the hay loft, I find myself thinking about how pale Annie looked at breakfast. A gnawing feeling deep in my gut tells me I should go check on her. She's been so excited these past few weeks as we neared our wedding day. But this morning, she seemed a bit preoccupied and rather subdued. It's probably nothing. It's probably just wedding-day jitters, but it wouldn't hurt for me to check on her.

I head for the ladder. "Hey, buddy, let's go check on your mama."

"Okay!"

I climb down first so I can spot Aiden as he scrabbles down the ladder. Then I make sure Frank gets down safely as well.

Aiden grabs my hand and pulls me toward the barn doors.

My dad opens the barn doors for us, and we step out into the chilly air. Frank hustles after us, his face flushed, and my dad brings up the rear.

4

Annie

Molly answers yet another knock on my bedroom door.

Jake's youngest sister, Lia, strolls in, her sharp gaze sweeping the room. "Are we having a secret girls-club meeting?" She props her hands on her hips. "And if so, why wasn't I invited?"

One thing I've learned about Lia McIntyre is that there's no telling what's going to come out of her mouth.

"We weren't excluding you, sweetie," Bridget says. "It was an impromptu meeting."

Lia studies her mother, who's sitting on the bed beside me. "All right, what's going on?"

"Annie might be in labor," Sophie says to her sister.

Lia's eyes dart from Sophie to me. "You're shitting me! Does Jake know?"

Bridget stands. "No, he doesn't. And don't you dare tell him." She looks around the room. "In fact, don't any of you tell any of the men. They're as thick as thieves. If you tell one of them, they'll all know."

At the sound of yet another knock, we all groan.

Molly opens the door, and there stands Sam Harrison dressed in ripped jeans and a form-fitting T-shirt that says, *I'm With Him*.

He surveys the room. "I'm looking for Beth—oh, hey, princess. Shane's looking for you. Luke had a blow-out. Is there a reason why you're all congregating in Annie's bedroom?"

"It's a secret girls-club meeting," Lia says. "You're not invited."

Sam arches a brow and cants his head imperiously. "Since when am I excluded from the girls' club? You know I'm an honorary member."

Molly pulls Sam into the room and closes the door. "Don't you dare tell a soul. Not even Cooper."

"Don't tell Cooper what?" Sam says.

"We think Annie's in labor."

"Oh, good Lord!" Sam bites back a smile as he comes straight toward me, reaching for my hands. "Are you sure?"

I nod. "Pretty sure. The contractions are coming about thirty minutes apart. They're not particularly strong or painful, but they're consistent."

Sam shakes his head. "Jake is going to flip his lid."

"Don't you dare tell him," Bridget says. "And don't tell Cooper, because you know he'll tell Shane, and Shane will tell Jake."

Sam nods. "True. They're worse than a bunch of magpies." He looks down at me. "What can I do to help?"

Before he can answer, there's a knock at the door. I smile when I hear a collective groan.

Molly opens the door, and there stands my mother.

"I'm looking for my daughter," she says as she walks into the room. "What's everyone doing in here?"

"Hello, Roberta," Bridget says, a genuine smile on her face.

Mom looks skeptically at Bridget, as if she's waiting for the punchline to a joke at her expense. When it doesn't come, she says, "Do you all mind if I have a word in private with my daughter?"

"Of course not," Bridget says, herding everyone toward the door. "Come on, girls. And you, too, Sam. Let's go check on... the catering."

After everyone leaves, Mom closes the door behind her and turns to face me. Dressed in a burgundy skirt suit with a white blouse and black heels, her hair pinned up in a severe chignon, she looks professional, aloof, and...cold.

"Mom—"

She crosses her arms over her chest and cuts me off. "Are you absolutely sure you want to go through with this wedding, Annie? It's not too late to call it off. Just because you're pregnant is no reason—"

"Stop!" I shoot to my feet. "I'm not marrying Jake because I'm pregnant. I'm marrying him because I love him! Why can't you accept that? What in the world do you have against him? He's a wonderful man, a fantastic father to Aiden, and he'll be an amazing father to our daughters."

Her lips flatten in a rigid line as her chest rises and falls rapidly.

"Why are you so against us being together? He's done absolutely nothing to make you dislike him so much."

She glares at me, tension radiating off her. When her chin starts to quiver, she abruptly walks to the window overlooking the sprawling lawn. She holds herself rigid, her arms crossed over her chest.

I join her at the window. "I'm getting married today to the love of my life. Why can't you be happy for me?" I risk a glance her way, and I'm shocked to see a tear rolling down her cheek. I've never seen my mother cry.

I lay my hand on her back, and I'm shocked to feel her shaking. "Mom, please. Talk to me."

She takes a shuddering breath as she raises an index finger to dab beneath her eyes, checking for mascara. "When I was eighteen years old, in my senior year of high school, I met a boy named Russell Parker. His family owned a small second-hand furniture shop in Lincoln Park. We started dating—secretly of course. My parents wouldn't allow me to go out on dates. We fell in love. A week before graduation, he asked me to marry him, and I said yes."

I'm stunned into silence because I've never heard this story before. I've never heard my mother mention any other men in her life before she married my father. And… I have to think back. She was just nineteen when she married my father. He was ten years her senior, already out of college and working for an accounting firm downtown Chicago. "You never told me this before."

She sighs. "What was the point? I married your father. My path was set."

"What happened? With Russell, I mean."

Another tear follows the first one, and she struggles not to cry. "My parents forbade me to see him ever again. His family wasn't the right sort of family. They said I'd be foolish to marry a shopkeeper's son. Instead, they arranged for me to marry your father."

My stomach drops like a stone, and I feel sick. "Arranged?"

She nods. "My parents handled all the arrangements. All I had to do was show up for the ceremony."

"But what about Russell? I thought you said you loved him."

"I did. But my parents refused to even consider him as a suitor."

"But—" My mind is racing as I try to make sense out of all this. "I don't understand. You were an adult. Surely you could make up your own mind about who you married."

"It didn't work that way, darling. Not back then. And not in my family. A week after I turned nineteen, I married Frank Elliot. Russell enlisted in the Army the next day and left town, never to return."

I shake my head as I try to process what she's saying. I always thought my parents were *happy*. I never once dreamed they weren't. A wave of dizziness hits me, and I'm so light-headed I have to sink into a chair before I fall down.

Mom frowns as she studies me. "Are you all right? You look pale."

I nod, not wanting to discuss my condition at the moment. "Whatever happened to Russell?"

"I never heard from him again. I did hear from a classmate that he'd married and moved to Florida."

"Does Dad know about any of this?"

She shakes her head. "I don't think so. At least I never told him."

My mind is reeling as I consider all the implications. She's been married for thirty-five years to a man she didn't want to marry. I never had any idea theirs was anything but a love match. My heart tightens painfully when I think about how she's put on a front all her life.

And then it dawns on me that she did to me exactly what her parents did to her, knowing how much it hurt. I meet her pained gaze head on, my own eyes tearing up. "And yet, you chose to do the same thing to me?"

She swallows hard and nods. "It was for the best, Annie. Back when you two were in high school, Jake was a ship without a rudder. He had no ambition, no drive. No way to support a family. Your father and I couldn't let you marry him. Yes, he's done well for himself since then, but we had no way of knowing how he'd turn out."

I'm shaking so badly I can hardly form a coherent thought. "That was never any of your business! I loved him, and that was all that mattered. You manipulated us!"

Her jaw tightens. "We did what we thought was best for you at the time."

"*We* did? Was this Dad's idea, too? Or was it your idea, Mom?" I shake my head in disgust. "You of all people should have known how much you were hurting me."

She stares defiantly out the window, refusing to meet my gaze.

"You were jealous!" I say, realization making me feel sick. "You didn't get the man you wanted, and you made sure I didn't get the man I wanted either."

As she turns to me, I see pain and a flash of guilt in her eyes. "Don't be ridiculous, Annie."

"It was all your idea, wasn't it? You made Dad go along with it."

"Frank has always been too soft where you're concerned."

"Then what does that make you? Hard? Hard-hearted? And you're proud of that?"

Something catches my mother's gaze outside the window, and she frowns. I move to join her and see Jake, Aiden, Calum, and my dad walking back from the barn. Aiden is holding the hands of both of his grandfathers.

"Do you resent Jake?" I ask my mother. "Do you resent us being together?"

She flinches, probably surprised I asked such a blunt question. But life's too short to beat around the bush. I learned that the hard way when Ted nearly killed both me and Jake.

Without looking at me, she says, "Yes."

Jake, Aiden, and the two grandfathers disappear from view as they enter the house. Their excited voices filter up the stairs from the foyer.

"Do you want to be part of our family?" I say. "If you do, you have to change your attitude. We're about to welcome two more children, and I will not let you poison my family with your resentment. You have a choice to make. It looks like Dad has already made his."

Loud voices come from outside my room, followed by a sharp little knock on my door.

I smile, knowing perfectly well who it is. "Come in."

The door swings wide, and Aiden races in. "Mommy, we saw the horses. I petted them! Daddy even let me sit on Giselle's back!"

Aiden throws his arms around me as best he can, despite my wide girth. He glances up warily at my mother, and it breaks my heart to see his hesitation.

"Hello, Aiden," Mom says.

"Hi, Grandma."

Jake comes forward and wraps me in his arms. He's brought in the chill from outside, and I shiver. "You're so cold!"

He laughs. "I need you to warm me up."

I glance past him to my dad. "Hi, Dad."

"Hello, honey." When Jake steps aside, my dad hugs me tightly. "You look beautiful, Annie. You'll be the prettiest bride there ever was."

I laugh. "The most *pregnant* bride, you mean."

As my father releases me, Jake pulls me back into his arms and touches his cold nose to mine. "I came in to check on you. Are you feeling okay?"

"I feel wonderful." That's the absolute truth. I do feel wonderful. I'm marrying the man of my dreams, and our family is growing. And no matter what comes our way, we'll face it together.

Jake ruffles Aiden's hair. "Hey, pal, why don't you show Grandma and Grandpa to the dining room so they can get some coffee?"

Aiden clasps his hands eagerly. "Can I have hot chocolate?"

Jake lifts a finger. "Just one cup. I think you've had enough sugar already today."

Once everyone's gone, Jake studies me. "Do you want to tell me what you and Roberta talked about?"

WITH THIS RING   33

My smile falls. "We talked about her attitude."

He scratches his short beard as he weighs his words. "And how did that go?"

"I told her she has a choice to make. If she wants to be part of our family, she needs an attitude adjustment."

He nods, seemingly satisfied. He's been really good about letting me handle my mother. Tugging a strand of my hair, he says, "How much longer now?"

For a moment, I think he's talking about the babies, and my pulse starts racing. But then I realize he's referring to the wedding cere-mony. "About two hours now," I say, mentally crossing my fingers. *I just need to make it two more hours.*

I know another contraction is going to come soon—I've been watching the clock. I don't want Jake here when it comes. "Would you do me a favor and get Sophie? I think we should start on my hair and make-up."

Jake drops a quick kiss on my lips. "I'll go get her. But I want to go on record saying you don't need any make-up. You're beautiful just the way you are."

I swat him playfully as he heads for the door.

A little while after Jake leaves our room, another contraction hits me, this one clearly stronger than the ones before. The air leaves my lungs on a ragged exhale as I drop down into the armchair in front of the window. Iron bands tighten around my middle, squeezing me, cutting off my air. This is escalating faster than I expected.

I do my best to breathe through it, taking slow, careful breaths and trying not to freak out. *I've done this before. I can do it again.*

"Come in," I say when I hear Sophie's quiet knock.

The door opens, and in walks Sophie and her mother.

Bridget takes one look at me and rushes over. "It's okay, darling," she says, kneeling on the rug in front of me. She lays comforting hands on mine. "Just breathe."

"Are they getting stronger?" Sophie asks.

I nod as I concentrate on breathing. Sophie and Bridget share a glance, neither of them saying a word.

Once the contraction eases, I lean back in the chair and blow out a long breath. "Let's do this," I say to Sophie. "Hair and make-up."

Bridget touches my cheek and smiles. "You'll be the prettiest new mother in the maternity ward," she says. "Hair, make-up, and a beautiful dress. Who else goes to such trouble before going into labor?"

5

Jake

After sending Sophie up to our suite to help Annie get ready, I go in search of my stepson. I find him in the kitchen, begging Elly for a second breakfast.

"I'm hungry again, Miss Elly," he says as he sidles up beside her at the sink. "Are there any more pancakes?"

She smiles at him affectionately. "You're a growing boy. Of course you're hungry. I'm afraid there aren't any more pancakes, but if you hold on a minute, I'm sure I can find you something."

"How about ice cream?" Aiden says, grinning hopefully.

She laughs. "Nice try, mister, but no. We're having cake and ice cream later today, after the ceremony. How about some fruit? I've got some fresh strawberries right here."

Elly sits Aiden down at the table with his bowl of strawberries.

I stand behind his chair, my hands on his shoulders. "Don't let him sweet talk you into anything."

"Don't worry," she says. "I'll keep an eye on him."

I leave Aiden in good hands and go in search of Cooper, who's going to officiate at our wedding. I find him in the great room, standing in his usual place... behind the bar, playing bartender. He's already dressed for the ceremony in a black suit and tie. A bunch of the guys are gathered around the bar.

I take a seat on the only available bar stool. "Hey, guys."

Shane claps his hand on my back. "Are you ready, little brother?"

"You bet I'm ready." I turn my attention to Cooper as he hands me a chilled soft drink. "How about you? Are you ready?"

Cooper jumped through the necessary hoops to get certified to officiate at weddings in the state of Illinois, so that he could marry Shane and Beth. Today, he's going to preside over our wedding.

"I'm an expert, son," Cooper says. He points at Shane. "I married this guy off, didn't I?"

My brother Jamie, seated on Shane's other side, offers me a toast with his water bottle. "Congratulations, Jake. I wish you all the happiness in the world."

"Thanks."

Sam joins us at the bar, sliding behind the counter to stand next to Cooper. He lays his hand on Cooper's back. "My man looks good all dressed up. Of course, he looks good no matter what."

The two men make a striking pair... Cooper with his short silver hair in a military buzz cut and the much younger Sam with his red hair gathered up in a manbun, piercings, and tatts.

Cooper shakes his head and grins at his partner. "Do you want something from the bar?"

"Nope. I just want to bask in the glory of your presence."

Cooper rolls his eyes and hands Sam a chilled soft drink.

Sam eyes the bottle with disdain. "Where's the beer?"

Cooper shakes his head. "After the ceremony. It's too early for booze."

It's good to be surrounded by family and friends on this very auspicious day. Annie and I are lucky to have so much love and support cheering us on. It makes up for Roberta's lack of support. I hope Annie's mom didn't upset her too much this morning. Annie looked rather pale.

I probably should go back upstairs and check on her again. I just can't shake this feeling that she's pretending to feel better than she does.

I hop off my barstool. "Here, Sam. You can have my seat."

As I pass through the foyer on my way to the staircase, Ingrid Jamison, Beth's mother, comes through the front door with her son, Tyler.

"Hi, Ingrid," I say, stopping to give her a hug. And then I offer my hand to Tyler. "Hello, Detective. Glad you could make it."

Tyler shakes my hand. "I wouldn't have missed it for anything. Congratulations on your big day, Jake."

"Thanks. Everyone's in the great room. Make yourselves at home."

I point up the staircase. "I'm going up to check on the bride."

When I reach the door to our suite, I knock. There's probably a passel of ladies in there, possibly getting dressed. Who knows what I might be walking in on.

The door opens, and Molly steps out into the hall, closing the door behind her. She leans against it like she's on guard duty. "Hi, Jake." She's a bit breathless, and her cheeks are flushed. "How can I help you?"

"I came to check on Annie."

"Oh, she's fine." Molly smiles. "She's kind of busy right now. Can I take a message?"

Molly's acting strange, and that only intensifies my concerns. "No message," I say. I debate forcing the issue, but I don't want to interfere with whatever the girls are doing in there. So, instead, I rap my knuckles on the door. "Hey, honey! Is everything okay?"

"Yes!" Annie calls back. "Everything's fine. We're just getting ready."

She sounds a bit overexcited. "Call me if you need anything, okay?"

"Okay!"

Molly gives me an expectant smile, but she doesn't open the door until I'm halfway down the hall. I jog down the stairs and go looking for my mom. She usually knows what's going on, but she's nowhere to be found. I can't find Beth or any of my sisters, either.

I return to the guys congregating around the bar in the great room. Shane's now holding his son, Luke, who is trying to climb up onto Shane's shoulders. I reach for Luke and set him on my shoulders, and he squeals his little head off as he clutches my hair.

"How'd it go?" Cooper asks me. "Everything okay upstairs?"

I shrug. "I'm not sure. I didn't actually get to see her. She's seques-tered in our suite with her female entourage. I did yell through the door, and she said she was fine." I turn to Jaime. "Molly was acting kind of strange, though. Hey, Jamie. Would you mind going upstairs and talking to Molly? See if Annie's really okay?"

Jamie sets down his bottle of water and rises from his seat. "Sure."

Gus, Jamie's service dog, jumps to his feet and positions himself next to Jamie. My brother grabs the dog's harness, and they head off.

Dad walks into the room, passing Jamie on his way out. When he joins us at the bar, he reaches for Luke. "Here, give me my grandson."

$\backsim$ 6

Annie

Only one more hour to go. I can do this.

I keep repeating that in my head as I pant through my next contraction, biting my lip in an effort to remain quiet. The contractions are getting stronger, and I'm starting to wonder if this is a really bad idea.

We all jump at the sound of yet another knock at the door.

Molly jumps up from her seat. "I'll get it."

"Who is it?" I ask quietly, peering across the room just as Molly slips out into the hall and closes the door behind her. I hope it's not Jake again, coming to check on me. I'm feeling guilty enough as it is hiding the fact that I'm in labor.

Bridget sits beside me at the foot of the bed, holding one of my hands in both of hers. My hair is done, swept up into a beautifully intricate knot decorated with tiny sprigs of baby's breath flowers. My dress is ready, but I want to wait to the last minute to put it on in case my water breaks. I don't want to ruin my dress before I've had a chance to wear it.

Everyone is on pins and needles as we wait for Molly to return.

She slips back into the room, closing the door behind her. "It was Jamie. I think he suspects something's going on."

"What did you tell him?" Bridget says.

Molly gives us all a guilty smile. "Well...he asked me a direct question—if there's something going on—and I couldn't lie to him. I'm sorry, Annie, I just couldn't."

"It's all right," I tell her. "I understand. Really, I do. If Jake asked me a direct question, I wouldn't be able to lie to him either." I heave myself up onto my aching feet. Now that the cat is out of the bag, it's only a matter of time before Jake comes barging into this room. I glance at the digital clock on the nightstand. The ceremony is scheduled to start in forty-five minutes. "Beth, would you mind helping me put on my dress? It's time."

I barely have time to shrug off my robe and slip on my dress before there's a sharp knock on the door. Actually, it sounds more like a fist pounding on the door. Before anyone can respond, the door crashes open and my soon-to-be husband stalks into the room. He's livid.

Forty minutes.

Jake's gaze zeroes in on me with the accuracy of a laser beam. He's a bit flushed, as if he ran all the way up here. His gaze narrows on me. "What's going on?" Without taking his eyes off me, he says, "Do you ladies mind? I'd like a private word with Annie."

"Suit yourself," Lia says as she saunters past him, followed by the others. "But just remember, it's bad luck to see the bride before the wedding."

Once they're gone, Jake shuts the door and comes right to me. "What the hell's going on? Talk to me, Elliot." He looms over me, his hands on my shoulders. He looks ready for battle.

"I'm okay, Jake, really. Just let me sit down for a minute."

His brow furrows as he watches me lower myself gingerly to sit at the foot of the bed, one hand on my lower back, the other on my abdomen.

"Annie." It's obvious he's not buying it.

"I've had a few contractions this morning," I say, choosing my words carefully. "It could be nothing."

He crouches in front of me so that we're eye to eye. "Or, it could be something. Are you in pain?"

"Not pain, really. It's more like a lot of pressure right now."

His hands slide up to frame my abdomen. "We should call your doctor."

I lay my hands on his. "I know what she'll say. She'll tell me to go to the hospital. I promise, once the ceremony is over, we'll go. We're getting married in half-an-hour. I don't want to miss that." Tears spring into my eyes. "Please, Jake. This ceremony is important to me. It has to be *today*."

He sighs. "Honey, the ceremony is just a formality. We're already husband and wife as far as I'm concerned."

"I know, but I want us to be husband and wife in the eyes of Illinois. I want to make it official, *before* our daughters are born. And you know it has to be today."

"March fifth. I know." As he brings my hand to his mouth for a kiss, I watch the battle being waged. He's fighting between giving me what I want and keeping me safe. He stands and sweeps me up into his arms, before sitting on the bed and holding me on his lap. For a moment, I feel surrounded in comfort and safety.

My abdomen begins to tighten. "Oh, no."

"What is it?"

I press my face against his T-shirt and pant through it. This is the strongest one of all, and it steals my breath. This one... hurts.

Jake's hand cups the back of my head, his fingers sinking into my hair. His other arm wraps securely around me, holding me to him. "Jesus, baby, why didn't you tell me?"

"This is the worst... one... so far." My words are muffled against the fabric of his shirt as I tuck into him.

His arms tighten around me, and I feel his lips in my hair. With a shock, I realize he's shaking.

As the contraction eases, I sit up and take a deep breath.

"Annie—"

"No, Jake, please. I *need* to do this. The ceremony starts in just a few minutes. Please, let me do this, and then we'll go to the hospital. I was in labor with Aiden for eighteen hours. I'm sure there's plenty of time."

He frowns, muttering something under his breath. Clearly, he's not happy.

I stand and smooth my dress with shaky hands. "I need to finish getting ready. Go get yourself and Aiden dressed, please."

He stands and pulls me against his chest, his arms wrapping around me. He towers over me, a giant of a man, clearly a head taller. "You're going to be the death of me," he says grudgingly. He grips my chin and tilts my head so that I'm looking him right in the eye. "You call for me if the situation gets dire, is that clear?"

I nod, tears welling up in my eyes. "I will. I promise." I reach up to stroke his cheek above his trim dark beard. "I've waited nearly half my life for this day, Jake. I can't miss it."

Grimly, he nods. "Let's make it quick then. My wife is not giving birth in the back of an ambulance."

Jake opens the door, and out in the hallway stands my entire entourage all dressed in their wedding attire: my sisters-in-law bridesmaids; Beth, my matron of honor; and the groom's mother. Jamie is there, too, along with Shane and Jason Miller. I join Jake at the door, slipping my hand into his.

"She's in labor," Jake says, cutting to the chase. He squeezes my hand.

Shane gives me a recriminating look. "You should have told us, Annie."

I straighten, my shoulders going back. "I'm not missing my own wedding."

Shane glances at Jason. "You're on stand-by."

The dark-haired, tattooed medic nods. "My medical kit is out in the truck."

I don't know Jason well, but I do know he delivered Beth's premature baby under difficult conditions. Shane openly credits Jason with saving Luke's life. He's a former paramedic, turned bodyguard now, and working for Shane. His specialty is guarding medically fragile clients.

"Mommy!" Aiden comes barreling around the corner. "Is it time to get married? Elly said I need to get my wedding clothes on."

I smile. "Yes, sweetie, it's time. Go with Jake and change into your suit."

Jake gives me a stern look as he cradles my face. "I'm going on record to say I don't like this. You call for me if you need me, is that clear?"

I nod. "Yes."

"I mean it, no heroics. You call for me."

"I will." I nudge him in the direction of the room where all the men will be getting dressed. "Go get ready."

Reluctantly, Jake heads down the hallway with the rest of the men's party, and Aiden.

Bridget shoos me back into my room. "Are you ready?"

I nod. "As ready as I'll ever be."

Sophie tidies a few strands of my hair that Jake must have knocked loose. She looks me over, apparently approving of what she sees. "Okay, you're ready."

Gentle strains of a guitar and cello duet waft upstairs from the great room. Jonah Locke, Lia's fiancé—who just happens to be a world-famous singer-songwriter—is graciously providing the music today. A friend of his who plays cello is accompanying him. I find the faint sounds of classical music soothing.

My mother walks in, her scrutinizing gaze sweeping the room. For a moment, her gaze lands on me, revealing nothing of what she's feeling. Then she nods perfunctorily at my future husband's mother. "Hello, Bridget."

"Hello, Roberta," Bridget says, smiling cautiously.

My mother has that effect on people. She puts everyone on edge because they don't know what she's going to say or how she's going to act. I just wish she could relax for a change.

I hear my dad's voice out in the hallway. "Annie, honey? We're ready to start if you are."

Bridget opens the door to let him in.

I lift my skirt and square my shoulders. "I'm ready."

* * *

As my father walks me down the staircase, we're accompanied by the bridesmaids, Beth, Bridget, and my mother.

I peek into the great room and see Cooper standing across the room in front of the windows. He looks very debonair in his dark suit.

But I only have eyes for Jake, who's standing next to Cooper. He's magnificent in his black tuxedo, crisp white shirt, and peach colored tie and cummerbund. Pinned to the lapel of his jacket is a pale peach boutonniere that matches my bouquet.

His dark gaze locks on mine. I can almost hear the question in his mind... *Are you all right?*

I give him a smile and a nod. *I'm fine.*

The groomsmen are already lined up beside Jake: his eldest brother Shane, along with his two other brothers, Jamie and Liam, and their dad, Calum. The McIntyre men make a formidable sight in their black tuxes, from silver-haired Calum to the youngest, Liam.

"Everyone, line up!" Sophie says as she hands me my bouquet. She gives me a gentle side hug. "You only have to hang on for a few more minutes."

"Thank you, Sophie, for everything." I don't know where I'd be without her.

"Mrs. Elliot, you're first," Sophie says, motioning for my mother to step forward.

A handsome young man with sandy brown hair and a clean-shaven face steps forward and offers his arm to my mother. "Mrs. Elliot, may I escort you to your seat?"

"This is Philip," Sophie says, gently pushing my mother in the young man's direction.

"Mom, you're next." Sophie waves another young man over, a handsome young Latino. "Miguel will escort you."

"Now the bridesmaids." Sophie waves her sisters closer. "Hannah and Lia, stand right here."

Lia steps forward and adjusts the bodice of her dress. "My God, this thing itches! Can we please get this over with so I can change?"

Sophie bites her lip to keep from laughing. "Beth you're next, after Hannah and Lia. And last, but not least, Aiden. Come here, sweetie."

Bouncing with excitement, and looking adorable in his pint-sized tuxedo, Aiden steps forward with a cream-colored silk pillow clutched in his hands. In the center of the pillow, our wedding bands are secured with a delicate peach ribbon.

Sophie lays her hand on Aiden's head. "You know what to do, Aiden, right?"

He nods gravely. "I give the wedding rings to Daddy, and then sit down next to Grandma Bridget."

"That's right." Sophie pats him on the head. "Just like we practiced yesterday, okay?'

"Okay!"

At the rear of the line, my father stands at my side, a beaming smile on his face.

Jonah and the cellist begin playing my procession song, the quintessential *Canon in D Major.* Their rendition is slow and lilting and simply divine. My chest floods with emotion and my throat tightens. *It's really happening!* I'm marrying my best friend, the man of my dreams. Suddenly all the years of misery, of being separated from Jake and tied to an abusive man, fade into the background.

My mother glances back from her position at the front of the procession. "Annie, stop crying. You'll ruin your mascara."

Sophie leans close and whispers, "You look absolutely perfect."

As the bridal party enters the great room, all the chatter ceases and everyone in the small audience turns to face us. Folding chairs set up on both sides of a center aisle are occupied by friends and family and employees of McIntyre Security.

I recognize quite a few faces... Killian Deveraux and Cameron Stewart, who are part of Jake's surveillance team. Mack Donovan and his girlfriend, Erin. Sam, of course. Elly and her husband, George. Beth's mother and her brother, Tyler.

The procession begins, my mother walking down the aisle first, then Bridget, followed by the bridesmaids and Beth, then Aiden. Aiden glances back at me as he starts walking, a gleeful smile on his face.

And then it's my turn. My father offers me his arm, and he escorts me down the makeshift aisle to the front of the room. Behind Cooper, the windows overlook a lawn that slopes down to the wild, untamed shores of Lake Michigan. It's a private and secluded setting, the perfect backdrop to one of the best days of my life.

Jake stands directly in front of me, across the spacious room, next to Cooper. He's an imposing sight, tall, broad chested, his dark hair and beard trimmed neatly. His gaze is still locked intently on me.

I smile, hoping to reassure him, but he doesn't relax even a little bit. This is the man who threw himself in front of me when Ted fired his gun. He took a bullet for me, without hesitation. The fact that his body slowed the bullet is the only reason I didn't die that day.

I do my best to smile serenely as I walk down the aisle. All eyes are turned on me. I think back quickly, trying to recall when I had my last contraction. Another one is due any time, and I just pray we can get through the brief ceremony before it hits.

Dad and I stop in front of the wedding party and turn to each other. He smiles at me. "I'm so happy for you, honey." His eyes tear up, and he struggles to maintain his composure. "Jake is a good man, and I couldn't be happier to call him my son-in-law."

He kisses my cheek and then hands me over to Jake before taking his seat beside my mother.

Jake draws me to his side and whispers, "Everything okay?"

I nod, giving him a tremulous smile.

The ceremony begins, and it's very straight forward. Jake and I tweaked the standard vows to fit us. He promises to love, honor, and cherish me for the rest of my life. I promise to do the same for him.

It's not until Jake slips the wedding band on my finger that my next contraction hits...*hard!* I double over with a cry, grasping my abdomen as the air rushes out of me. My body feels crushed in a vice, and I'm struggling to catch my breath.

As warm liquid streams down the insides of my thighs, I glance up at Jake, trying not to panic. "My water broke."

Jake swings me up into his arms and starts moving toward the exit. Our guests come up out of their chairs, and concerned voices fill the room. My mother shoots to her feet, visibly upset, and my father does his best to calm her.

Bridget rushes to my side, keeping pace with us, and takes my hand. "Everything's going to be okay, darling. Just hang on." Then she glances up at her son. "You're taking her to the hospital?"

Jake nods curtly, not wasting his breath with an answer. He's moving fast, a man on a mission.

Jason Miller runs ahead of us, clearing a path to the front door.

"I now pronounce you husband and wife!" Cooper yells after us from half-way across the room.

"Damn right we are," Jake mutters, making me laugh in spite of myself.

"Mommy!" Aiden cries.

I clutch Jake's shoulders. "What about Aiden?"

Jake doesn't miss a step. "My dad has him, honey. Don't worry, he's fine."

Lia's there ahead of us in the foyer, holding open the front door. She gives her brother a pointed look. "I told you it was bad luck to see the bride before the ceremony."

Out front, Jake's black Tahoe is parked in front of the doors, the engine running. Killian Deveraux is sitting in the driver's seat.

Jason opens the rear passenger door, and Jake slides into the vehicle, cradling me on his lap. Jason takes the front passenger seat.

"Go!" Jake says to Killian.

I'm painfully aware that my wedding gown is soaked through, and I'm sitting on Jake's lap. "I'm ruining your clothes."

"Don't worry about that," he says gruffly as he gently settles me on the seat beside his and fastens my seatbelt. "I brought us both a change of clothes."

"You planned all this?"

"Of course I did." He lays his hand on the firm mound of my abdomen. "I wasn't going to leave anything to chance. Are you in pain?"

I wince, because yes, I am. The contractions are getting steadily stronger. I pant through it. "A little."

Jason reaches back from the front seat to grasp my wrist, his fingers pressed to my pulse.

When the contraction finally passes, I sigh in relief and sink back into my seat.

As we drive down the long lane to the main road, I barely register the scenery as it flashes past me...the pasture on our left, horses gathered on a slight rise, the pond on our right.

"The hospital is twelve minutes away," Jake says, as he checks his watch. "This is faster than calling an ambulance."

My heart is hammering in my chest, and I'd be lying if I said I wasn't afraid. Having a baby is a big deal—even more so when there are two of them. So many things can go wrong. I've done this before, but still, it's unnerving. And if the tension radiating from Jake is any indication, he's just as anxious as I am. He's just better at hiding it.

I lean my head back on the headrest and close my eyes. *Just breathe. You can do this.*

Jake reaches out to gently stroke my hair. "We'll be there in ten minutes."

Even without looking, I know he's turned in his seat to face me, his attention focused on me. I'm in good hands, and so are our babies. He'll make sure of it.

7

Jake

I've done a lot of scary shit in my life, but nothing has ever shaken me like this. Annie—my wife of ten whole minutes—is in labor.

There's not enough time to get her back to Chicago, so Killian drives us to the local hospital in Kenilworth. It looks like the babies will be born here in town.

My attention is focused one hundred percent on Annie. Killian will get us where we need to be, and Jason is monitoring Annie's condition. All I have to do is focus on *her*.

I lean close to kiss her temple. She feels warm to the touch, perspiring lightly, but I imagine that's to be expected. Her body's in distress.

God, I hate the idea of her hurting, even for a moment. "Everything's going to be okay," I say, as much for myself as for her.

After shucking off my jacket and tie, and tossing them in the back, I undo the top two buttons of my shirt. Then I lay a hand on Annie's abdomen, which is rock hard. When I feel one of the babies kick, I can't help but smile. I'll be able to hold that little thing in my arms in just a matter of hours. I don't know whether to be excited or terrified.

Just as we pull up to the hospital admissions door, another contraction seizes Annie. Her entire body tenses, and she grabs my hands and squeezes tightly. My heart about stops when she lets out a whimper of pain.

I unbuckle Annie's seatbelt and lift her into my arms. "Hang on, honey. We're here."

Jason opens my door and I slide out of the vehicle, Annie held securely in my arms. Still in the middle of a contraction, Annie scrunches her face up tightly, her eyes closed. I'm not even sure if she's aware that we've arrived.

Jason leads the way as we storm through the automatic doors into the admissions area. He takes care of the details while I concentrate on Annie. A moment later, a female staff member brings over a wheelchair and I sit Annie down carefully.

"And you are?" the woman asks me.

"I'm her husband." *God, it feels good to say that.* "Jake McIntyre. And this is my wife, Annie. She's in labor, with twins."

She nods. "I'll take her to labor and delivery. If you would sign her in at the Admissions desk...."

Shaking my head, I reach for the chair handles. "I'm not leaving my wife."

"I'll take care of the paperwork," Shane says, appearing suddenly at my side. He claps a hand solidly on my shoulder. "You take care of Annie. I've got this."

When I glance back to see my entire family standing inside the entrance, a surge of emotion hits me hard. They're all here for us. "Where's Aiden?"

"He's back at the house with Beth and Elly," Shane says. "He's fine."

I push Annie's wheelchair to the labor and delivery ward where we're assigned a room. A nurse is already waiting for us inside. The delivery room looks more like an upscale hotel room than a hospital room, with floral wallpaper, a sofa and two armchairs. The bedframe is mahogany.

"Let's get her out of that dress," the nurse says.

I help Annie to her feet. Then I strip off her wet dress and undergarments as the nurse dresses her in a hospital gown. As I lay her on the bed, another nurse arrives, and the two of them hook Annie up to several monitors.

"How far along is she?" the first nurse asks me.

"Thirty-eight weeks."

"And how long has she been having contractions?"

"Since breakfast," Annie says in a breathless voice. "About five hours."

She's flushed, her face red and damp with sweat. I do my best to make her comfortable as the nurses work quickly and efficiently.

After hooking her up to a blood pressure monitor and oxygen meter, one of the nurses examines Annie to see how much her cervix has dilated.

"Seven centimeters," the woman says as she removes her gloves. She smiles. "You got here just in time, honey."

There's a flurry of activity after that point, one nurse taking Annie's vitals and recording the information. Someone else comes into the room to hook up Annie's IV and to draw a vial of blood.

I can tell Annie's scared. Her dark eyes are wide as she takes everything in, but she says nothing.

"Do you want an epidural?" the nurse—Kelly, according to her name tag—asks her.

Annie nods shakily. "Please."

Jason comes into the room carrying our overnight bag, which he sets down beside the sofa. "I brought everything in from the SUV," he says as he joins me at Annie's bedside. He smiles at Annie, reaching down to pat her leg. "How are you doing?"

She smiles weakly. "Good."

My mom joins us a moment later, taking a seat next to the bed. She reaches for Annie's hand. "I'd like to stay, if you don't mind."

Annie nods eagerly. "Thank you. I'd like that."

It's too bad that Annie's mom isn't here with her. Annie had asked her several times if she wanted to be here for the births, but Roberta never gave her a firm answer one way or the other. And based on the fact that the woman's not here now, I don't have much hope that she'll come. But my mom's here. She wouldn't miss this for the world.

The room is quickly prepared for the arrival of twins—two bassi-nets are rolled into the room, one labeled 'Baby McIntyre A,' and the other one designated 'Baby McIntyre B.'

The contractions continue, coming faster and harder. Annie seems like she's in her own world now as she deals with the dis-comfort. Someone comes to administer her epidural, and once that starts taking effect, it helps tremendously.

The rest of the afternoon is a blur, one contraction followed by another. Dr. Williams, the obstetrician on-call, comes in several times to check on Annie and monitor her progress. The two labor and delivery nurses coach Annie through the contractions.

An hour later, with Dr. Williams standing at the foot of the bed, Annie starts pushing. I'm on one side of the bed, and my mom is on the other. I position myself so that Annie's looking right at me, and I hold her gaze. There are tears in her eyes as she strains until she's red in the face.

I hold her hands in mine, keeping her focused on me, trying to give her strength. I'd bear all of this for her if I could. It kills me to see her so distressed, to know she's enduring this all on her own.

Thirty minutes later, our first daughter is born. Once her head and shoulders are clear, she slides quickly into Dr. Williams' hands. I stare down at the baby, whose face is pinched and blue.

"Is that normal?" I say, staring at the baby. "Is she breathing?"

But Dr. Williams seems perfectly calm as she picks up the baby and rolls her onto her side, rubbing the baby's back. She uses a bulb syringe to clear the baby's airway. A moment later, when the sounds of an infant's breathy cry fill the air, I suck in air. I didn't realize I'd been holding my breath waiting to hear her cry.

Nurse Kelly offers me a pair of surgical scissors. "Here you go, Dad. Would you like to cut the umbilical cord?"

"Me?" *Shit.* "Are you sure?"

Kelly grins at me. "Yes, I'm sure. You can cut the cord."

I take the scissors from her and carefully cut exactly where she points. Then Kelly lays the baby on a table, wipes her down, weighs her, and then lays her in bassinet A. She puts an identification bracelet on the baby's ankle, as well as a matching one on Annie's wrist. I'd be quite content to stand next to the bassinet and stare at my baby, but there's no time. Baby B is about to make her appearance, and Annie needs me.

After the second baby is born, I get to do the honors again by cutting the cord. I watch this baby get wiped and weighed and tagged.

While the two delivery nurses tend to the babies, Dr. Williams finishes up with Annie. I stay at Annie's side, holding her hands, but my attention is split between my wife and the two little babies lying in bassinettes across the room.

Two baby girls. Good Lord! I have two daughters. How is that even possible? A year ago, I was a bachelor, and now I have a family of five. It's kind of hard to wrap my mind around it.

I gaze into Annie's flushed face. She looks a bit frazzled, as one would expect. I lean forward to kiss her sweaty forehead, and then I look her directly in the eyes. "I'm so damn proud of you."

She gives me a relieved smile. "Thank you." She peers over at the bassinets. "Are they okay?"

"They're perfect, if you don't mind them wrinkled and purple."

She laughs. "All babies look like that when they're first born. Can I see them?"

The attending nurses bring the babies over and place them on Annie's chest, side by side, so she can hold them against her skin.

I stare in awe at the tiny babies with their wrinkled skin and caps of dark hair. Their eyes are closed, their faces scrunched up, as they fret and fuss. Studying them, I search for differences between them, but I can't see any. They look identical to me. *How the hell are we supposed to tell them apart?*

Annie looks exhausted, but happy. I brush her damp hair back from her face.

She glances down at the babies as she cradles them close. They've both settled down, and I suspect they've dozed off.

"They're perfect, aren't they?" she says.

"Yes, they are. And so are you."

She laughs. "I'm a horrible, hot mess, and I know it."

I gaze down at the babies, who are currently still covered in remnants of slime. Their dark hair is matted to their heads, and their eyes are closed. I'm expecting to feel terrified any minute, to panic at the thought of being responsible for three kids, but I don't. I feel... centered. This is *my family*.

I watch with fascination as Annie attempts to latch one of the babies onto her breast. The baby certainly gets top marks for effort. She's going at it eagerly, if not quite successfully. It takes some patience, but finally the baby latches on and attempts to suckle. After a while, Annie works with the other baby and helps her latch on. I can tell this is going to be a process, probably one of many.

"It'll be a couple of days before your milk comes in," Mom says. "But keep nursing them. This colostrum is good for them."

Annie and I have been discussing names for months now, since we found out we were having girls. I point to baby A, who's currently nestled in the crook of Annie's arm, fast asleep, her little cheek pressed against Annie's breast. "So, this one is Emerly, right?"

Annie nods. And then she smiles at baby B. "And this is Everly."

"This might be a stupid question, but how are we supposed to tell them apart? They look exactly the same to me."

She grins. "We could write on the bottoms of their feet in permanent marker, label them."

"You're kidding, right?" I honestly can't tell. I'm part horrified at the suggestion, and part intrigued. Frankly it sounds like a good idea. In the military, we labeled damn near everything.

She shrugs. "It's either that or paint one baby's toenails. I suppose that would be a more elegant solution."

I shake my head, a big fat stupid grin on my face. I'm still not sure if she's pulling my leg or not. "Aiden's going to flip out."

8

Annie

The two nurses swaddle the babies in blankets and wheel them out of my room to be bathed and officially assessed by a pediatrician. I grab Jake's arm. "Go with them! Don't let them out of your sight, not even for a second."

"I'm on it."

He follows them from the room, right on their heels, clearly a man on a mission. Once they're gone, I sink back in bed, so exhausted I can barely move a muscle.

"Is there anything I can get you?" Bridget says. "Do you want some water?"

"Not right now, thank you. I just want to rest for a few minutes." My vagina is throbbing and swollen, and the epidural has long since worn off. I'm feeling every painful twinge.

Bridget reaches for my hand. "They're beautiful, Annie. Thank you for giving me two beautiful granddaughters."

I sigh, just glad it's over and the babies are finally here. "You're welcome."

I'm grateful that Bridget is here with me. She's been amazing, the way she has embraced me and welcomed me into her family. I just wish I could say the same for my own mother.

Right now the only cloud hanging over my head is my mother's attitude. I had hoped my marriage to Jake would thaw her a bit, or perhaps the birth of her granddaughters would, but I don't see signs of that happening anytime soon.

I understand her so much better after she told me about Russell, and I'm so sorry for her loss, but it doesn't excuse her behavior. Yes, her parents ruined her happiness, but that doesn't give her the right to ruin mine. And as for my dad... he's caught in the middle. I don't know how much he knows about Russell, if anything. I don't think any of this is his fault.

I close my eyes, taking these quiet few minutes to rest. I'm sure the babies will be back soon and wanting to try to nurse again. It's been a few years since I've nursed a baby. Hopefully it's like riding a bike, and you don't forget how.

Bridget quietly gets up from her chair and walks to the door. I hear soft whispers out in the hallway, female voices. When I open my eyes, Bridget pokes her head through the doorway. "Beth is here with Aiden. Is it okay if they come in?"

"Of course!"

Beth walks in holding Aiden by the hand. My son watches me warily from a few feet away, and then he scans the room. "Did you have the babies?"

"Yes, I did. Come here, honey." I hold my arms out to him, and he rushes forward and climbs up onto the bed.

"Careful, Aiden," Beth says, hovering over him. "Don't climb on your mommy."

"Where are they?" Aiden asks me.

"The nurses are giving them a bath. They'll be back soon."

"Where's Daddy?"

"He's with your sisters."

"Oh." Aiden snuggles close to me, wrapping his arm around my pudgy belly. "I was scared when you cried at the wedding."

"I'm sorry, honey. I'm fine. There's nothing to worry about."

Before long, the nurses wheel the bassinets back into the room, Jake right behind them.

He gives me a thumbs-up. "Everything looks good."

The nurses park the bassinets at the foot of my bed, side by side. Aiden crawls to the end of the bed and peers inside the cradles at his sleeping sisters. "Which one is which?"

Jake does the honors, pointing at one baby, then the other. After checking their wristbands, he says, "This is Emerly, and this is Everly."

"They have nametags?"

Jake laughs. "Yeah. It's pretty near impossible to tell them apart."

He reaches out to muss Aiden's hair. "So, what do you think, pal?"

Aiden frowns. "They're so little. They can't even play."

Jake laughs. "Give them time. They'll be running circles around you before you know it."

When it's time for them to go, Aiden gets teary-eyed as he clings to me. "I want to stay here with you."

Jake picks Aiden up. "Come here, buddy. You stay with Aunt Beth and Uncle Shane tonight, okay? Hopefully, we'll all get to go home in a day or two."

We kiss Aiden good-night and send him off with his aunt, back to Shane's Kenilworth home. Bridget goes with them, leaving Jake and me alone with our babies.

Jake hands me one sleeping baby, and then another, and he climbs in bed beside me and we all cuddle. The babies are nestled against my chest, and Jake wraps his arms around all of us, holding us securely.

The babies do look remarkably the same, and I wonder if they're identical. I'm thinking they might be. They both have a good amount of dark hair, and they both have adorable little button noses and tiny rosebud mouths. They're both petite, weighing in at just under six pounds each, and they're practically swallowed up by their matching newborn sleepers.

I study them, mesmerized. "Can you believe this?"

"It's going to take some getting used to." He kisses my cheek. "Thank you for marrying me today."

I melt against him, reveling in the heat of his body. "Better late than never."

He pulls me close. "You were magnificent today."

I laugh. "Yeah?"

"Yeah. But next time, don't wait so long to tell me you're in labor. We cut it pretty close today."

I groan. "Please don't talk about a next time quite yet. I'm still recovering from this one."

* * *

The next day and a half fly by quickly. Jake never leaves my side, and we have a steady stream of visitors... Jake's family, our friends, and Jake's co-workers. I personally thank Killian Deveraux and Jason Miller for getting us here so quickly.

The babies are actually doing pretty well. They're napping a lot and trying hard to nurse. They pass their physicals with flying colors.

I spend my time attempting to nurse the babies and taking cat naps whenever I can. When I wake up from one of those cat naps, I'm surprised to see my mother sitting beside my bed. She's holding one of the babies in her arms. "Hi, Mom."

She glances up at me. "I hope I didn't wake you."

"No, you didn't. I've been napping on and off all day." I look around the room. "Where's Jake?"

"I offered to sit here with you and the babies while he went down to the cafeteria with Frank to grab a bite to eat."

"That was nice of you. He's been glued to my side since we got here, and I'm sure he could use a break."

Mom gazes down at the baby in her arms. "This one is Everly. She started fussing, so I picked her up. I didn't want her to wake you."

I watch my mom with great interest. I don't think I've ever seen her so relaxed, and I don't ever remember seeing her hold a baby. "I'm glad you could come."

She looks up at me, suddenly very serious. "I've been thinking about what you said to me yesterday, when we were talking about Russell and Jake. You accused me of hurting you the same way my parents hurt me. And you asked me why I resent Jake so much."

My heart starts hammering painfully, and I'm almost afraid to hear what she has to say. "Yes."

She diverts her gaze back to Everly, gently stroking the baby's hair. "Jake waited for you. He didn't move on. He didn't get married and start a family with someone else."

"And Russell did?"

"Yes. Just a year later, he got married and moved to Florida."

"Does Dad know about Russell? About what your parents did?"

"He didn't know for a long time, not until after you were born. We ran into some of my high school friends at a party, friends who knew Russell, and they told me he'd remarried. I reacted badly to the news. Later your father asked me about Russell, and I told him."

"What did he say?"

"Your father offered me a divorce, if that's what I wanted. I told him no. At that point, it didn't matter anymore. Russell was married and had children, and I didn't want the stigma of a divorce hanging over me." She shrugs. "What I wanted just didn't seem to matter anymore."

My heart is breaking, not just for my mother, but for my father as well. They were both victims.

"Frank is a good man, Annie. Never doubt that. He's always been a faithful husband and a good provider. I'm sure I don't deserve him, but nevertheless he puts up with me. And that business with you and Jake, that was all my doing. Your father just went along with my wishes. But I'm sure you've figured that out by now."

"Hello, ladies," my dad says from the doorway. "I hope we're not interrupting anything."

"Not at all," Mom says.

Jake walks into the room, his gaze lighting on me. "I went downstairs to get a bite to eat. Everything okay?"

I smile at him, genuinely glad to see him again. "Yes, fine."

He walks to the bassinet and picks up Emerly. Then he comes to me and leans down to kiss my forehead.

Mom looks up at him, her expression inscrutable. "They're fine babies, Jake. Congratulations."

I don't know who is more surprised by my mom's unexpected compliment: me, Jake, or my dad.

* * *

Just as we're getting ready to take the babies home, I lay them on the bed to change their diapers and put them in clean sleepers.

"Oh, my God, what's this?" I say when I spot a tiny black dot on the heel of Emerly's foot.

Standing on the opposite side of the bed, packing up baby supplies, Jake grins guiltily. "I just wanted to be sure."

"You wrote on our daughter?" I'm trying hard not to laugh. "Please tell me you didn't use a permanent marker."

He shrugs as he tucks diapers into the diaper bag. "Don't worry. It'll wash off eventually."

"Eventually?" Now I can't help laughing. Jake is pragmatic, if nothing else.

I finish changing Emerly, and then I do the same for Everly. When they're dressed and ready for the short journey home, I lay them side by side on the bed and study them. They really do seem to be identical. I'm finding it hard to tell them apart. Perhaps Emerly's face is a tad bit rounder than Everly's, but it's hard to be sure. Everly might have a tiny bit more hair on her head, but that's going to change quickly.

Jake walks up behind me and wraps his arms around my waist, drawing me to his chest as he peers over my shoulder. "We make pretty babies, don't we?"

I grin. "Yes, we do."

Once we're ready to go, Jake brings the Tahoe up to the front entrance, and then he comes to my room to get me and the girls and wheel us to the vehicle.

Aiden is already back in Chicago staying with Jake's parents, who live right next door to us in the McIntyre family gated compound. I've missed him terribly. I just want to get home and have my family together under one roof.

It's just a half-hour drive home along a very busy highway, but the entire time, my attention is riveted to the backseat, where the infant car seats are installed. Both babies sleep through their first car ride.

After pulling the SUV into our garage, Jake carries both car seats into the house while I hobble in slowly behind him, carrying the diaper bag.

He stands holding both car seats, one in each hand. "Where do you want them?"

"In our room, please. I need to lie down, and they can sleep in their bassinets."

Jake follows me to our room and lays both girls in their bassinets. While I'm changing into comfortable PJs and climbing into bed, he goes next door to collect Aiden from his parents' house.

I'm half asleep when I hear Aiden whisper loudly to Jake, "Is Mommy sleeping?"

"Yes. Shh, don't wake her. It's hard work having babies. She's very tired."

It's quiet for a moment, and then Aiden whispers, "Do they sleep all the time?"

"Pretty much," Jake says.

The mattress dips gently as both of my guys climb onto our big king-sized bed. Aiden snuggles between the two of us, his arm going around my waist. Jake gently strokes my hair. "Are you awake, Mrs. McIntyre?"

"Mmm hmm."

"Go to sleep. Aiden and I will hold down the fort."

9

Jake

Watching Annie now, with our girls, is very satisfying... the way she flits around diapering and changing and rocking and nursing. When they cry, she coos at them and they immediately stop. She makes it look so damn effortless. When I handle them, I'm always afraid I'll hurt them, they're so tiny and fragile.

The babies still look exactly the same to me. I couldn't tell them apart if my life depended on it... not without cheating and looking at the bottoms of their feet. Emerly's still got the black dot on her right heel. I reapply it every few days when it starts to fade. Annie laughs at me because I won't let her remove it. But excuse me... I'd like to know which of my daughters is which.

We've taken to dressing Emerly in pink and Everly in anything that's not pink, just to keep them straight. Aiden swears he can tell them apart, and when I quiz him, he gets it right every time. Maybe the kid's onto something. But when I ask him how he knows which one is which, he just shrugs and gives me a *duh* face. I suspect having kids is going to make me prematurely gray.

My mom comes over every day to help out around the house. She's been cooking for us and cleaning, rocking babies, burping, and changing diapers. I offered to hire someone to do the housework, but she wouldn't hear of it. She's in her happy zone taking care of family.

Dad's been helping out, too, with outside chores like shoveling snow and taking out the trash. My primary job is to keep Aiden entertained and change diapers. I took eight weeks of parental leave from work so I could stay home and be useful.

"I'll just pop this casserole in," Mom says, as she slides a baking dish into the oven. "Our guests should be here any minute."

There's a quiet knock on the front door, and Aiden races past me. "I'll get it!"

I follow him down the hall to the foyer, where a small crowd has gathered. It looks like the entire penthouse crew is here. Shane and Beth are taking off their coats, as are Cooper and Sam.

I reach for my nephew. At nine months of age, this little towhead is sturdy, so I'm less afraid of denting him. "Hey, guys! I'm glad you could make it. Come on in and have a seat." I unzip Luke's coat and pull it off, along with his hat. "Mom's got dinner in the oven."

We all head to the great room to sit and relax. Aiden invites Luke to sit on the rug and play cars. These two have become best buddies, now that Luke has become a bit more mobile, crawling around and attempting to stand. My nephew is a helluva cute little kid with his pale blond hair and blue-green eyes. He's a little pint-sized version of his mama.

Luke crawls over to the sofa where Cooper and Sam are seated, and he grabs hold of Cooper's jeans and pulls himself up to a standing position. He holds his hands out to be picked up, and Cooper sets him on his lap.

Mom joins us. "Dinner will be ready in twenty minutes." She bends down to kiss the top of Luke's head, stroking his hair. Then she smiles at Cooper and Sam. "You two would make great parents. Have you thought about that?"

"That's what I keep telling him!" Sam says, stealing Luke away from his partner. "He'd be an awesome dad."

Cooper laughs. "I'm a bit old to become a first time dad."

"Nonsense!" Mom says. "You're never too old. Besides, kids will keep you young."

With a bit of help from Sam, Luke walks across Sam's lap and back onto Cooper's. Cooper reaches out to steady him. Since Cooper and Sam live with Shane and Beth, they're more or less auxiliary parents to Luke.

"We're not even married yet," Cooper says.

Mom dismisses that excuse. "Then set a date and get busy."

Beth laughs. "That's what I've been saying!" And then to me, she says, "Where's your wife?"

"She's in our room, nursing the babies. I'll let her know you're here."

I head down the hallway toward the bedrooms and slip into our room. Annie's seated in an upholstered rocking chair that sits beside the bed, Everly cradled in her arms. Emerly's in her bassinet, wide awake, kicking her legs and flailing her arms.

I pick up Emerly, holding her against my chest, and sit on the side of the bed facing Annie. "They're here."

"I know. I heard Aiden greeting them at the door."

I watch, mesmerized, as Everly suckles eagerly at Annie's breast. The whole miracle of life thing and nursing just blows me away. Women are capable of doing amazing things.

I get off the bed and kneel beside the rocking chair, holding Emerly next to her sister. Sometimes it's overwhelming to think that we're responsible for the lives and happiness of two little girls.

I glance up at Annie, whose chocolate brown hair hangs over her shoulder. She meets my gaze with a smile. *Damn.* She's glowing. My chest tightens. I'd heard that women were often emotional after giving birth, but I didn't realize that I would be too.

"What's wrong?" she says, suddenly frowning as she watches me.

When I blink, I'm surprised to find my eyes are wet. *Shit.* "Nothing's wrong."

Annie lays her hand against my cheek. "It's a lot to process, isn't it?"

She thinks I'm overwhelmed by the babies, but it's not that. It's way more than that. When I think about how close I came to never having this moment... to never having Annie in my life again, it scares the shit out of me.

If her first husband hadn't been such a fucking bastard, we'd never have found our way back to each other. If her father hadn't hired McIntyre Security to protect Annie from her stalkerish ex-husband, we might never have gotten back together. I might have lived the rest of my life without her. Without *this*. *My own family*.

"Annie—" My voice breaks as I struggle to find the right words. I don't know how to tell her how much she means to me. Saying *I love you* just isn't enough. I swallow hard, floundering. I wish I was better at this.

She smiles, her own eyes suspiciously damp. "I know. I love you, too."

I wrap my arms around the three of them, *my girls*. I'd slay dragons for them. I'd do absolutely anything for them, and for Aiden.

An eager knock at the bedroom door diverts our attention.

"Come in," Annie says.

Aiden comes into the room and joins our little huddle at the rocking chair, sliding beneath my arms to be included. He puts his arms around his mama. "Grandma says dinner will be ready soon." He looks curiously at me, then at his mom. "Why is Daddy crying?"

Laughing, I wipe my cheeks with the hem of my T-shirt. "Sometimes, when you're really happy, you just gotta cry, buddy." Then I stand and, with Emerly resting in the crook of one arm, I take Aiden's hand. "Let's go visit with our company. Mommy will be along shortly."

So, Emerly and Aiden and I head to the great room.

As soon as we appear, Beth's out of her seat, making a beeline for the baby. "Can I hold her?"

I hand Emerly to my sister-in-law, who cradles my daughter to her chest.

Beth looks up at me with a bashful smile. "Who am I holding?"

"That's Emerly," Aiden says as he drops down onto the rug to play with his toy cars.

Beth looks to me for confirmation, and I shrug. "Don't look at me. He's always right. And yes, this is Emerly."

Beth sits next to Shane on the sofa and coos at the baby.

Mom sits down on her other side and reaches out to touch Emerly's dark hair. "Have you two given any thought to another baby?" she says, glancing up at Beth and Shane.

With a grin on his face, Shane lays his arm across Beth's shoulders. "Well, since you mentioned it...."

Mom's eyes grow big. "What!"

Beth nods. "We're expecting again."

Mom presses her hands to her face and beams. "Oh, good Lord, are you serious?"

"I'm almost three months along now," Beth says. "We're due at the end of September."

Shane holds his hands out for Emerly. "We didn't want to say anything until after Annie and Jake's babies were born."

Mom shakes her head in disbelief. "I've gone from zero grandkids to four in less than a year, and now soon to be five."

"Five what?" Dad says, as he walks in through the door to the garage. He's dressed in a heavy winter coat and gloves, his short gray hair and broad shoulders dusted lightly with snow.

My mom jumps excitedly to her feet. "Beth's expecting again, honey."

"You don't say!" He walks over to Shane and shakes his hand. "Congratulations, son." And then to Beth, he says, "When are you due?"

"Late September," she says.

Annie walks into the room holding Everly. "Did I just hear you're expecting?" she says to Beth.

Beth lays her hand on Shane's thigh. "Shane's convinced we're having a girl this time."

Annie props Everly on her shoulder and pats the baby's back, trying to get a burp out of her. "Do you want to know what you're having?"

"No," Beth says. "I think we'll let it be a surprise this time."

"It's a girl," Shane says with certainty as he leans close to kiss Beth.

Mom grins at Cooper and Sam. "You two had better get busy, that's all I'm saying."

ॐ **10**

Annie

After our company leaves, I lie down and rest while the girls are napping. Despite having just given birth to two babies, I feel pretty good. I'm tired, yes, but my body is bouncing back much quicker than I expected.

The bassinets are positioned right beside the bed, so I can lie on my side and watch the babies sleeping. It's amazing how different everything is this time around, with an attentive father. When I had Aiden, Ted showed little interest in our son. He seemed to resent the baby for taking up so much of my time and attention. Jake, on the other hand, is a wonderful father, most especially to my son, who's feeling a little left out lately. He may not be Aiden's biological father, but Jake clearly loves my son as much as any father could.

The door opens quietly, and Jake slips into the room. "He's asleep." Jake has taken over the evening routine of putting Aiden to bed.

"Do you mind some company?" he says as he kicks off his shoes.

"Of course not." I hold my hand out to him, and he takes it as he crawls onto the bed.

Jake slips beneath the covers and nestles up against me, tucking into my backside and slipping his arm around my waist. "They're both asleep?"

"Yes." I cradle one of his hands against my chest and lean down to kiss it.

His hand is huge, dwarfing mine. Like everything about him, it's big and strong and so capable.

He proceeds to trail kisses from the sensitive spot behind my ear, down the side of my neck, to my shoulder. "Have I told you lately that I love you?"

"Not in the last hour, you haven't."

He chuckles. "Then I've been remiss." He kisses my cheek. "I love you."

I roll over to face him. "I love you, too."

He kisses me, his mouth warm and gentle on mine. "Thank you for giving me three great kids. I'm a very lucky man."

It amazes me that Jake takes so much pleasure in being a father. Ted saw it as an obligation, as an imposition. I remember when Ted grabbed Aiden's forearm and shook him so forcefully that Aiden's tiny radius bone snapped like a twig. Aiden wasn't even two years old at the time. I still remember the sound of the bone cracking, as well as Aiden's screams of pain. I shudder.

Jake pulls back sharply. "Hey, what's wrong?"

I shake my head. "Unpleasant memories, that's all. It's in the past."

He draws me closer. "Tell me. If something hurt you, I want to know about it."

I squeeze my eyes shut against the sting of burning tears. "Ted got mad once when Aiden wouldn't stop crying. He grabbed his arm and shook him so hard Aiden's arm bone snapped in half. That's when I knew I had to leave him."

Jake's arms tighten on me. "Jesus. I wish I could shoot that fucker all over again. He got off way too easy for all the harm he caused."

I slip my hand up beneath his shirt to stroke his strong back, firmly kneading his heavy muscles.

He groans as he presses his face into the crook of my neck. "God, Elliot."

When one of the babies starts fussing, Jake rises up on his elbow to peer into the bassinet. "That's Emerly. I'll get her." As he stands over her bassinette, he makes a face. "She pooped." He picks her up and cradles her to his chest as he carries her to the changing table.

"Do you need help?" I ask him.

"No, I've got this."

And then he painstakingly changes her diaper, just like I showed him how, and redresses her. She's wide awake now, so he brings her back to bed with him and lays her between us.

Emerly wriggles, drawing her knees up to her chest and flailing her tiny fists. She squeaks and squawks a bit as she works her way up to a good cry.

"Babies are so helpless," he observes as he watches her.

When Jake reaches down to gently stroke Emerly's cheek with the tip of his index finger, she turns her face toward him and opens her mouth wide.

He laughs. "Sorry, young lady. I can't help you there. That's your mama's job."

I roll to my side to face her, unbutton my top, and unclip the cup of my nursing bra. "Here you go, sweetie."

Jake rolls to his back with a low groan. "Some people have all the luck."

Epilogue

Annie

I t's been eight weeks since the girls were born. Eight blissful weeks of playing house, changing diapers, having Jake home all the time. After I divorced Ted, I left my job at my father's accounting firm, and I haven't started back to work since. I'm not sure if I'm going to go back at this point. It's nice being home with the babies and Aiden, and Jake told me I don't need to work if I don't want to.

Summer is here, and it's beautiful outside. We spend a lot of time outdoors, going for walks, playing at the park. Jake is overseeing the addition of a small pond on the property, and I'm looking forward to seeing ducks and turtles frolicking in the water.

This family compound is really coming together nicely. Only

three other families live here besides us—Jake's parents, Beth's mom, and Lia and Jonah—but we're hoping others will join us, especially Shane and Beth, Sam and Cooper, and perhaps Jamie and Molly.

It's nice to be able to go outside and wander around without any worries. This gated community has on-site security around the clock. There are often a few fans loitering outside the gates, hoping to catch a glimpse of Jonah, but the guards keep them from causing too much trouble.

In the playground across from our house, I sit with two napping babies on a blanket under the shade of an oak tree and read while Aiden climbs on the jungle gym.

I glance up when I hear a slight sound. "Hi, Lia."

Lia's dressed in black work-out gear, and her blond hair is braided.

"Are you heading to work?" I ask her.

"Yeah. I'm teaching a martial arts class this week at the office." She sits down on the blanket and peers over me at the babies, who are sleeping side by side, nestled together like baby bunnies. "They're growing."

I nod. "Yes, they are." I catch sight of the slender gold band on Lia's ring finger. She and Jonah got engaged a few months back, but there's been no mention of a date. "Have you guys picked a wedding date yet?"

Lia frowns as she shakes her head. "Jonah keeps pestering me about it. 'Pick a date,' he says. 'Any date.'"

"Why haven't you?"

She shrugs. "My folks have been married for ages. I just can't imagine anyone putting up with me for that long. I have trouble putting up with myself from one week to the next."

My heart breaks for her. She's such a strong young woman in so many ways. She's lethal in the fighting ring, she's a formidable bodyguard, and yet she's so lacking in the self-esteem department. "Jonah adores you, Lia. He wouldn't have asked you to marry him if he didn't want to spend the rest of his life with you."

She frowns. "It's a slippery slope. If I marry him, then he's going to want kids. He goes on and on about your kids and Luke all the time. I know he's going to want some of his own."

"And you don't?"

She shrugs. "It's not that I don't want them. It's just that I'd be a terrible mother. I'm not like you and Beth. You guys make it look so easy. Even with all her problems early on, Beth has turned out to be a fantastic mother. And you? You're like the perfect mom."

Aiden yells from the playground. "Lia! Can you help me?" He's perched at the very top of the jungle gym, staring down warily at the ground far below. "Help, I'm stuck!"

She climbs to her feet. "Hold your horses, kid. I'm coming."

Bridget joins me on the blanket, and we both watch Lia climb up the jungle gym to rescue Aiden.

"Lia thinks she'd make a terrible mother," I say, my heart hurting for my youngest sister-in-law.

Bridget shades her eyes as she watches Lia rescue her grandson from his high perch. "Lia always underestimates herself. She's a strong, capable young woman who can do anything she sets her mind to. She'd be a great mother. All my girls would."

After setting Aiden on the ground, Lia waves to us as she heads across the street to her own house.

"Where's she going?" Bridget says as Lia climbs into her Jeep.

"To the office, to teach a martial arts class."

Bridget frowns. "I wish she could slay her own demons as easily as she slays the bad guys."

* * *

That night, after putting the babies in bed for the night, I head into the bathroom to brush my teeth and get ready for bed. Earlier that day, I shaved my legs and underarms, tidied up my eyebrows, and moisturized from head to toe. I even painted my fingernails and toenails with Jake's favorite shade of red. I've done everything but hang a sign over our bed. *Open for business!*

I love my husband to pieces, but enough is enough! Dr. Shaw gave me the go-ahead to resume having sex two weeks ago. I've been dropping hints ever since, but Jake seems determined not to notice. Since he's far from stupid, he must be doing it on purpose. I think he's just being overly-cautious. And that needs to stop, right now. I want to have sex with my husband!

Jake's in the shower, and the steamed-up glass shower door does absolutely nothing to block my view of his tall, muscular body standing under the spray of hot water.

Dressed in a short, sheer nightgown, I watch him unabashedly through the semi-fogged glass. Those long, soapy fingers glide briskly over his broad chest, and over the contours of his biceps and heavily inked arms. He soaps his chiseled abdomen, his sturdy haunches and buttocks, and finally his long legs.

When he reaches between his legs to wash his genitals, my brain short-circuits. *Good grief. Enough is enough!*

The Chippendales have nothing on my Jake. If he ever got tired of the security business, he'd make a fortune as a stripper.

The water shuts off and he opens the shower door to reach for a towel. He grins at me. "What are you smiling about?"

I bite my lip. "Nothing."

He steps out of the shower to dry himself. "Really?"

"Yes, really." And then—God knows where I find the courage to do this—I pull my nightgown up over my head and let it slide to the floor. As naked as the day I was born, I saunter out of the bathroom and back into our bedroom.

I barely make it halfway to the bed when he's right behind me, his body warm and damp from his shower. He scoops me up into his arms and carries me to our bed, depositing me gently in the center of it. Then he crawls onto the bed, on his hands and knees, and looms over me, caging me in. My body responds instantly with a surge of heat, and my sex clenches tightly. I can smell the scent of his heated skin, his soap, and good, clean maleness.

He sweeps one hand down the side of my torso, over my hip, and around to the back of my bare thigh. "Do you want to tell me what this little show is all about?"

Grinning, I wrap my arms around his neck. "I'm pretty sure you can guess."

His gaze darkens and his damp skin flushes. "Honey."

"It's been two months, Jake. I'm fine. I told you, Dr. Shaw said—"

"I don't care what Dr. Shaw said."

I thread my fingers through the short strands of his hair. "Come here." And then I pull his face down to mine and kiss him in such a way that he couldn't possibly misunderstand me.

"Annie—"

And to seal the deal, I reach between us and wrap my fingers around his penis, which is already fully erect, and stroke him from root to tip, teasing the crown. He's thick and hard, his body clearly on board. But his head… that's a different story.

With a pained expression, he lowers his forehead to mine. "I'm afraid I'll hurt you."

"Oh, sweetheart." I cup his handsome face in my hands and bring his mouth back to mine for a kiss. "You won't hurt me. I promise you, I'm ready."

He reaches between my legs, gently cupping my sex. "Are you absolutely sure?"

He sounds so uncertain, I have to chuckle. "Yes, I'm sure. Believe me, I wouldn't even suggest it if I wasn't."

I press his fingers more intimately against me, and when he feels how wet I am, he groans. "Jesus, you're going to kill me."

I open my legs wider, inviting him closer. Tentatively, he slides a finger between the lips of my sex, then hesitantly tests my opening by gingerly inserting one finger. His touch alone sends my nerves reeling.

I groan in anticipation. "Jacob McIntyre, you'd better make love to me right now, or else!"

He presses his lips to mine. "Do you realize this will be our first time since we became husband and wife? The pressure's on now."

I laugh, opening my legs even more. "I wonder how many men have to wait two months before consummating their marriage?"

He kneels between my thighs and leans forward to kiss me. "I waited *years* for you, Elliot. Two months is nothing."

He trails kisses down my throat, over the swell of one breast. He flicks my nipple with the tip of his tongue, making it peak hard into a tight rose-colored bud. When a tiny bead of milk appears, he licks it off. "I have a whole new appreciation for your breasts."

I swat him playfully as he continues lower, his lips teasing me as they skim further down my belly. He nuzzles my soft, rounded belly, then dips down to tickle my belly button with the tip of his nose.

Finally, he reaches his destination and flicks my clitoris with his tongue.

I bite back a cry. "Oh, God!"

When he starts in on my clit, I grasp his broad shoulders, holding on for dear life. He's voracious, a master of oral sex, and he always makes me come first. He licks and suckles and teases me until my body is strung like a tight wire, poised for release. His finger slips gently inside my opening, and when he finds my sweet spot, he cautiously strokes me.

"Jake." My voice is breathy, my limbs trembling. Everything he's doing—his tongue, his touch—it all feels so good. And it's been *so* long.

Relentlessly, he strokes me deep inside while his tongue torments my clitoris. He's tenacious, unyielding, as he drives my arousal higher and higher. I'm panting now, trying to keep quiet, which isn't easy.

The last thing I need to do is wake up one of the babies.

Pleasure swells deep inside me, rising like a wave of sensation about to crest. My hands are restless on his shoulders, my nails digging into his muscles, then they're in his hair, gripping the strands tightly. He growls deep in his throat, a sure sign of his own pleasure building. He likes to feel my hands on him, my nails digging into his muscles, my fingers pulling his hair.

My climax hits me hard, and I press a pillow to my face to muffle my cries. My hips buck over and over against his mouth, but he doesn't let up. He keeps pushing me higher and higher, making me tremble and shiver and quake. Gasping for air, I toss the pillow aside and breathe in, taking in the mingled scents of our heated and aroused bodies.

As my body comes down from the high, he rises over me, on his hands and knees.

He wipes his mouth and beard on the sheet, then leans down to kiss me. "Tell me if this hurts."

"Mmm." I'm still reeling from my orgasm, too caught up in rippling waves of pleasure to respond coherently.

He grasps my chin and locks onto my gaze. "I mean it, Elliot. If anything hurts, you tell me."

I kiss his hand. "I'm fine. Stop worrying."

He scowls, clearly not satisfied with my response. But nevertheless, he reaches into the top nightstand drawer and pulls out a condom. Sitting back on his haunches, he rolls the condom onto his thick shaft. Then he's looming over me once more, his erection in hand. Watching me closely, he feeds his erection into me, a bit at a time.

I love that he cares about my comfort, but I'm feeling impatient at the moment. I want to feel him inside me, filling me, stretching me. I love having that connection with him. I love watching his face and his body as he moves inside me, chasing his own pleasure.

He takes his sweet time rocking gently, his expression taut. I clasp his heavily muscled arms and sink my nails into him to encourage him to move faster. But he's calling the shots here, and there's no rushing him.

Finally he sinks the last little bit inside me, until he's fully seated, and I gasp. It's a snug fit, but I love it. He's not really hurting me, but I am highly aware of his size.

"Are you okay?" he says, his voice rough with desire and tension.

I nod, biting my lip as my body adjusts to him. I dig my nails into his biceps and rock my pelvis against him, trying to encourage him to move.

"Take it easy," he says. "We're not rushing this."

It's all I can do not to laugh because the tables are turned right now. He's usually the aggressor, but right now our roles have flipped. I just want to feel him moving inside me. I want to feel his strength and his passion. And he just wants to be careful.

He starts moving, so slowly, gently gliding all the way out, then sinking slowly back in. He sets up a steady, soothing rhythm that feels wonderful. The head of his erection drags deliciously through my sheath, teasing my nerves. My hips rock against his thrusts, meeting him move for move, and it feels so good! He's hitting me at just the right angle, brushing against my g-spot with each thrust, and I feel on the verge of a second orgasm. It's rare for me to come twice, but I think I'm so worked up, and so hungry for him, that it just might happen.

His mouth locks onto mine and I can feel the tremors wracking his body, the harsh breaths soughing in and out of his lungs. He's holding back because he's afraid of hurting me, when he really wants to let go and thrust hard.

I dig my nails into his buttocks and clench down on him, bucking against him as I urge him to move faster, harder.

"Elliot, stop," he mutters against my mouth.

I bite his lower lip and smile. "Make me."

"Ah, fuck!" He rears back and thrusts inside me, so hard and deep that my head bumps the headboard. "Shit! I'm sorry."

I laugh. "I'm not. Now stop talking and start fucking."

His eyes widen in surprise at my choice of language. I'm sure he's never heard me say that word before. "Yes, ma'am."

Levering himself up on his hands, he looms over me, dark and beautiful, as his hips begin a powerful, thrusting rhythm. His face contorts with pleasure, and he bites back a groan.

My nerves explode deep inside me, sending out wave after wave of pleasure with a startling and rare second orgasm. He lowers his mouth to mine and drinks in the keening sounds coming out of me.

When my sex tightens on him, squeezing him hard, he tenses, his head arching back, his back bowing. He grimaces with pleasure as his climax hits him. I stare up at him, in awe of his sheer physical power. The tendons in his neck and shoulders are pulled taut, his face flushed with exertion.

When he opens his eyes and meets my gaze, I'm stunned by the flash of vulnerability I see in him. For all his incredible strength, he's as shaken as I am.

As his orgasm wanes, small tremors continue to wrack his big body, and his arms tremble. He lowers his mouth to mine and kisses me gently, reverently. "God, I love you."

He rolls carefully to my side, turning me with him so that we're facing and still joined. My arms go around his waist, and I kiss his chest. "I love you, too."

His heart is hammering in his chest as he draws me close, still buried deep inside me. "Is this okay?"

"Yes."

"I didn't hurt you?"

"No, you didn't." Truthfully, I am a bit sore, but he doesn't need to know that. If he knew, he wouldn't be in any hurry to repeat this, and after two months of celibacy, I am ready for more.

He tightens his arms around me and kisses my forehead. "You're going to be the death of me, Elliot."

I nuzzle my nose in his crisp chest hair. "I'm Annie McIntyre now, remember?"

He laughs. "You'll always be my Elliot."

And then he kisses me like he means business.

The end… for now.

Coming Next!

Stay tuned for more books featuring your favorite McIntyre Security characters! Watch for upcoming books for Tyler Jamison, Sophie McIntyre and Dominic Zaretti, Hannah McIntyre and Killian Deveraux, Liam McIntyre, Charlie Mercer, Cameron and Chloe, Ingrid Jamison and Joe Rucker, and many more! There are so many books in my head and not enough hours in the day!

For updates of future releases, follow me on Facebook or subscribe to my newsletter. I'm active daily on Facebook, and I love to interact with my readers. Come talk to me on Facebook by leaving me a message or a comment. Please share my book posts with your friends. I also have a very active reader group on Facebook where I post weekly teasers for new books and run lots of giveaway contests. Come join us!

You can also follow me on Instagram, Amazon, BookBub, and Goodreads!

Visit my website: www.aprilwilsonauthor.com.

Please Leave a Review on Amazon

I hope you'll take a moment to leave a review for me on Amazon. Please, please, please? It doesn't have to be long... just a brief comment saying whether you liked the book or not. Reviews are vitally important to authors! I'd be incredibly grateful to you if you'd leave one for me. Goodreads and BookBub are also great places to leave reviews.

Acknowledgements

As always, I owe a huge debt of gratitude to my sister, Lori, for being there with me every step of the way. Her tireless support and encouragement are priceless.

Thank you to my personal assistant, Julie Collier. I never realized how much I needed a PA until Julie started making my life easier.

Thank you to Sue Vaughn Boudreaux for her unwavering support. With her many excellent skills, Sue is invaluable.

Finally, I want to thank all of my readers around the world and especially the amazingly kind and wonderful members of my reader group on Facebook. I am so incredibly blessed to have you in my life. Your love and support and enthusiasm mean the world to me. You've become dear friends to me, and I am grateful for you all. Thank you from the very bottom of my heart for every review, like, share, and comment. I wouldn't be able to do the thing that I love to do most—share my characters and their stories—without your amazing support. Every day, I wake up and thank my lucky stars!

With much love to you all... April

Made in United States
North Haven, CT
16 November 2022

26814321R00064